PRIME CHOICE

PRIME CHOICE

STEPHANIE PERRY MOORE

Dafina Books for Young Readers
KENSINGTON PUBLISHING CORP.
http://www.kensingtonbooks.com

DAFINA BOOKS are published by

Kensington Publishing Corp.
850 Third Avenue
New York, NY 10022

ISBN-13: 978-0-7582-1863-6
ISBN-10: 0-7582-1863-X

Fist Kensington Trade Paperback Printing: July 2007
10 9 8 7 6 5 4 3 2 1

Printed in the United States of America

For my hubby, Derrick

Thanks for making the choice to share your life with me.
Seeing you play, coach and motivate others has made
football my favorite sport.
Watching you help young men reach their full potential
inspired me to do the same!
May every reader know pleasing God is the best decision
they'll ever make.

Acknowledgments

For years, I've written books where the main character has been a female. Several male readers challenged me to write from their perspective. After much prayer, research and work, I'm excited that the Perry Skky Jr. series is finally here. I hope it gives insight to my female readers and encourages my male readers.

Simply put, I know the teen years can be hard. Drama on every side. If it ain't one thing it's another. Well, I pray this series meets you where you are and helps you to know that God is with you through it all. Everybody needs a little help now and then. And here's a special thank you to those who helped me reach another goal.

To my parents, Dr. Franklin and Shirley Perry Sr., I'm blessed to have you. One can't choose one's parents, but if I could I'd make no changes.

To my publisher, Kensington/Dafina Books, and especially my editor, Selena James, I love your heart for this series. You came on board and took this one under your wing. Thanks for helping the series soar.

For my writing team, Calvin Johnson, James Johnson, Ciara Roundtre, Jessica Phillips, Randy Roberts, Ron Whitehurst, Vanessa Davis Griggs, Larry Spruill, John Rainey and Teri Anton, you helped me keep it real and get this out there. I'm so grateful that you looked this over to make sure I was on point with the story. The insight you gave to this project will help it reach more for Him.

To the special young men in my life, Leon Thomas, Franklin Perry III, Kadarius Moore, Dakari Jones, Dorian Lee, and Danton Lynn, I love you. I pray this series can help you along the way. Know that you will accomplish greatness for God.

To my little cheerleaders, Sydni and Sheldyn, thanks for being proud of Mommy. You'll soon be in high school yourself. May this book help you to understand the minds of boys.

To my new world of readers, thanks for trying this series out. Know that you can choose the right path always. Allow God to help you.

And to my Lord and Savior, thanks for giving this fun new series life. I've so enjoyed writing this story you placed in my heart. May every reader make the prime choice of surrendering their life to You.

Contents

~ 1 ~

Needing a Yes

"Come on, Tori, you know this feels good. Just say yes," I said as I kissed my girlfriend of two years on the ear.

When she pulled away, it ticked me off worse than I could describe. Why'd she lead me on? I had committed to dating only her for the past two years and now that we were into the third, it was time for her to put up or, dag, I'd have to move on.

"You're mad," she said as she bit her pretty fingernails.

The stare I gave her was cold. There was no need to answer her question. I had just gone from really wanting to be with her to wanting our relationship to be over. I mean, I didn't have time to play games. This is my senior year. I was a highly recruited wide receiver. The schools in the Atlantic Coast Conference and the South Eastern Conference wanted me badly. Every time I stepped into a party, girls were lining up to get with me. And here I was, trying to do the right thing. Wanting to be faithful to one girl. All for nothing.

Before I could make it to the door, Tori pulled me back into her arms.

"Perry, don't walk out like this. I love you. I'm just not ready. I know this is your last year in high school and all, but

I'm not ready for sex. You used to understand that. Why are you changing all of a sudden?"

I shrugged. "I got different needs now. I can't explain it. I just don't know. I'm tired of this game, Tori. I want your actions to speak louder than your words."

I went and sat back down on the couch and put my head down on my knees and tried to cool off. The girl needed to let me leave. She wasn't ready to do nothing. Maybe our relationship had gone as far as it could go.

I believed in God, but I wasn't really completely walking with the Lord. I was baptized in the sixth grade and felt that God and I had an understanding. Though He wanted me to remain pure until marriage, I believed He would be straight with the fact that I wasn't trying to sleep around like my crazy boys.

I wanted my first time to be with a girl I deeply cared for. I only wanted the best for Tori. I didn't want anybody to mess with her. I liked protecting her and having her around. Yeah, Tori Guice was the one I wanted to take things to the next level with, but she wouldn't let me. I lifted up my head when I felt her stroking the back of my neck.

Even physically I had changed a lot in the last year. My body had stretched from 6 feet 1 inch to 6 feet 3 inches. Everybody kept hollering at me, askin' when would I play hoops. But football was my thing. The extra height would be a plus to the new season, with me trying to impress all the college coaches. There wasn't too many defenders, corner backs or defensive backs that would be able to cover me on the field. I knew my extra height would give me an advantage to catch balls thrown high with my name on them. Even the track coach was on me to run in the off season.

Every aspect of my life was cool except this one. My older sister, Payton, would be out of my hair away at college in a bit. Actually, I liked her a lot more now than I did when she used to take up the bathroom space. She had much drama her senior year and I wasn't going there. My grades were good. I had five college visits set up in the next three months and had turned down five more. My dad had hooked me up with a two-door sports ride from his dealership. Life was on the up for the most part.

Yeah, Tori was a cutie and I wanted to stay with her, but she wasn't going to mess up my flow. *Now what was she doing?* I thought. She knew better than to stroke my head like that. She was making a brotha feel things that made my heart race fast. I turned toward her and kissed her passionately til she pulled away from me again.

"Perry, I thought you liked me for *me*. I thought you were okay with the fact that I didn't want to go all the way," she said as she fastened her pants I'd worked hard to unloose.

"Obviously you don't understand," I said to her as I got up. "I'm tired of being the bad guy for wanting my girlfriend to make me feel good. You know I'm a good guy. I don't mistreat you and I've never cheated on you. Reward me!"

I had been at her house for two hours and I had only intended to be there for about an hour 'cause we knew her dad would walk through the door at six. Now it was after six. And there Mr. Guice was—standing tall.

He squinted his eyes and surveyed the room. "Perry, I thought you were only supposed to drop my daughter off. Tori, is your mom home?"

I knew I was thrown up under the bus at that point (a saying my dad always used when trouble came his way). Maybe God was up there watching out for me. I couldn't imagine being caught in the position I wanted us to be in. Mr. Guice would have had my head for sure.

I walked toward the door. "Hey, sir, sorry, sorry. I gotta go."

"Nah, man, wait. Let's talk about the upcoming football

season. My daughter stressing you out?" he asked as he gave Tori a disappointed smirk.

It was always funny to me how fathers tolerated a little extra when their daughter was dating a guy they respected. I watched my dad do that with Payton's boyfriends, Dakari and Tad. Now Mr. Guice was playing that stuff with me. I mean, really, what did he think we were in here arguing about? Our clothes were on, but they weren't straight.

"Oh, Dad, you think it's my fault? Well, how's this? Your hero Perry Skky Jr. wants to have sex with me. Should I do that to keep him happy?" Upset, Tori walked right past her father and went outside.

Mr. Guice leaned so close up to me I could feel the fire in his heart. "Is what my daughter said true, son? I don't mind y'all having a kiss here and a hug sometimes, but we had an understanding. You promised me no lines would be crossed. You changing the rules on me?"

Boy, I didn't want to lie to that man. However, there was no way that I could tell him that some nights all I could think about was his daughter's chest, lips and thighs. I was raised in a good home. My folks taught me to be a cool kid but have respect for my elders. I wasn't a punk, but I wasn't a thug, either. My boys ragged me for not having sex sometimes, but I held my own so they knew not to take jokes too far. Actually, I think they appreciated my stance. How was I to answer Tori's dad?

"What's up? You can't even be man enough to tell me that you wanna take my daughter's innocence away?" he asked as I stood frozen before him. "I know. I remember what high school was like. So listen here, partner: I'm gonna let you walk out my house with all your faculties intact 'cause you gonna do one of two things—remember the rules of this game or play with another girl. Are we clear?"

"Yes, sir."

"Now, you go out there and tell my daughter to get her tail back in here, talking smart to me like she done lost her mind. I gotta set her straight, too."

"All right, sir."

I grabbed my keys and headed out the door. I had every intent of getting in my car, pumping up the music and cruising on home. I couldn't find Tori, though. When I did, she was in her backyard under the gazebo, crying. I cared too much for her to just stroll away.

When I sat down beside her and touched her hand, her eyes were closed but she knew it was me. As she fell into my arms, a part of me wanted to forget everything I wanted and stop wanting more. But was that realistic?

I prayed to God: *"Lord, this is hard. As I smell my girlfriend's sweet perfume, I want something from her that You tell me I shouldn't have now. I'm struggling and really need You to help me keep my feelings checked."*

"Perry, I'm sorry," she said, still sobbing. "I do wanna be with you. I know you could have anybody at our school and you want me. Ciara and Briana tell me all the time how I need to just put out."

"Listen to me, Tori," I said as I lifted her up off my shoulder. "I only want you if you want me. It ain't right for me to force you into doing it my way, and you shouldn't let your girls dish you into doing it the way they do, 'cause, trust me, my boys Damarius and Cole don't deserve them."

Tori laughed with tears still flowing. She knew how true that was. They were players and though I didn't agree with them being untrue to their girls, I couldn't stop them. That's why I guess I was so mad that Tori wasn't ready for us to go further. I wasn't planning to do her like that. Even though I wanted her in my life, we were at a gridlock. I had to end this.

Kissing her on the forehead, I said, "Tori, I don't want to

hurt you. You know you got my heart, but we want something different. I got to let this go for now, you and me."

"No, Perry, no! Please don't do that."

As if she wasn't already crying hard enough, she flipped out in a way I'd never seen. But I had never broken up with her before. Even though I was moved, I realized something had a hold on her that was making her not take it to the next level with me. I knew it was her Christian beliefs. How could I mess with that? I was struggling with letting God down myself. I had to leave her alone even though it was killing me to see her so sad.

"You'll always be special to me, though, Tori. Your dad wants you inside. Call me." Then I squeezed her hands, left the gazebo and drove away.

I wasn't in my room for five minutes when my crazy sister opened up the door without knocking.

"Hey, little brother. What's up?" she asked, too bubbly for me.

Payton had a couple more weeks before she went back to school at the University of Georgia. She and I had done a lot of fun stuff over the summer. We went white-water rafting on our family trip to California. We spent time sightseeing in DC. I actually enjoyed the Broadway play we saw in New York. My sister was the bomb, but at that moment I needed my space.

"Oh, so you don't wanna talk to me," she said, being her naturally obtrusive self. "I know when you shut your door somethin' ain't right."

"What you talking about?"

"Who's done something to you?"

"If you gotta know, I cut Tori off."

"Oh, I know what this is about. So it's like that," my sister said as she stood near my bed. "You think you're ready?"

"Guess so."

"Then I'm so glad Tori stood her ground. I'm going to just let you sit here and sulk about the mistake you just made."

As Payton shut my door, I knew she was right. I was already regretting my decision, but it was done and I was going to stand by it. I didn't need to be tied down, no way. This was my senior year and I was going to get *mine*. The Lord just needed to help me find out what *mine* really was.

Four days had passed. It was Saturday and I hadn't thought about Tori that much. I'd been working out, hanging with my boys, thinking about college and pondering my senior year.

I was in the car cruising with my parents and two of my tightest boys, Damarius and Cole. We were headed to Columbia, South Carolina, for USC's Football Fan Appreciation Day. South Carolina had wanted me to come to a game this season, but I was already scheduled to go to other schools on the days of the games they had designated for their top recruits. This event was the compromise. Coming to Fan Day was another way to get high school seniors excited about USC before committing to another university.

My boy Cole was being recruited by them as well. He really wanted to go there and be a Gamecock. Cole was 6 feet 1 inch, 260 pounds. He could run a five-three, almost unheard of for a defensive lineman. All that weight just seemed like it wasn't even on him when he was in full speed. The brother could tackle out of this world and his presence made quarterbacks tremble. With his C average grades it looked hopeful. If he passed the SATs, he would have no problem going to USC.

As much as Cole had it going on on the football field, his home life was shady. He and his mom lived in the projects. His dad was never there, his mom was on and off drugs. He was the oldest of four boys. He worked odd jobs to make ends meet. Though his mom had a car, it barely worked. So my dad was happy to take Cole with us on the trip.

My parents had really taken to both of my friends. All three of us were known in our school for dating these girls that all hung together and were a year younger than us. Tori, my girl, or rather my ex; Ciara, Damarius's squeeze; and Briana, the sweet, hefty sister that dated Cole. The three girls were like the three of us—always together—and oftentimes all six of us were together rollin' in a crew.

My other partner, Damarius, was off the chain. He was a straight nut. Always clowning. Though he acted like stuff didn't stress him, I knew a few things did. He hated the fact that his parents weren't married. His dad moved back in with him and his mom and didn't work nowhere. His eighth-grade sister got pregnant last year. He felt bad that he was happy when she miscarried. But it was a blessing. He wished more schools were recruiting him for football, but his grades and his talent weren't reeling in the big dogs.

I couldn't bring him on my recruiting trips because schools limited me on my guests. But since this wasn't an actual game, the USC head coach was cool with me bringing him. Damarius was such a loudmouth sometimes; I hoped he didn't embarrass me or Cole.

Damarius bragged, "Yeah, I'ma go tell that coach he got his eyes out on y'all and he needs to be lookin' out for me. I'm the brotha with the skills."

My father listened in from the front of the car. "Boy, if anybody is going to be talking to the coach, it's going to be me. We didn't bring you all the way up here to cut up."

"Honey, he was just playing," my mother said to my father.

"Yeah, Mr. Skky. I was just teasin'," Damarius replied as he gave me a look showing he was serious.

I was a little worried about my folks. The two of them had been acting strange this summer. My sister and I come in and out the house, so we don't see much of their interaction. However, when we had our family trip to New York, I could tell my parents weren't really feeling each other. They didn't say much to each other and when they did speak they were rude and cold.

I didn't know what their distance was all about. Payton had no clue either. Out of all my seventeen years of being in the house with them, they always worked through the tough times. So I hoped this would all blow over soon.

Finally, we had made the hour and a half drive to the stadium. We were greeted by the director of high school relations. Cole was off the chain excited. I had to admit, when we first walked into that stadium it was impressive. We went over to a booth that was set up for recruits. We stood up there with some of the top prospects in South Carolina. All eyes were on us at first because we were from Georgia. Word quickly spread on who we were. Cole jumped right in and started meeting people. Damarius stuck to me like glue. My parents went to a meeting with the athletic director and other parents.

I wasn't a shy guy, but when introduced to adults I was a little reserved and passive. So I didn't mind shooting the bull with Damarius a bit. There was a spread of food that filled four tables: catfish, fried chicken, slaw, cornbread, baked beans, green beans, French fries and brownies. Damarius and I tore up the meal. Cole finally came back to us wearing barbeque sauce all over his face.

"Man, fix yo mouth," Damarius yelled out.

"Oh, oh, my bad, my bad. Hand me something." I passed him a napkin. "I was coming over here to let you know about your competition. See that ol' tall, slim dude over there?"

Cole pointed at this tall, caramel-toned guy running his mouth. Both Damarius and I nodded to acknowledge we saw who he was talking about. Then I shrugged my shoulders.

"Hold up, Perry. That's Saxon Lee," Cole said as if I was supposed to give the guy major respect.

I had never met the dude, so I had nothing against him. Even though he was South Carolina's top wide receiver and I was said to hold that position in my state, I felt there was room for both of us on the next level. Saxon didn't intimidate me. As a matter of fact, I'd heard he was cocky and from seeing him love the attention from all the other recruits I could tell some of the rumors I'd heard about him were true.

"Oh, snap, look at his girl," Damarius said. The three of us switched our attention to the hottie standing close to Lee. "Oh, yeah, that's mine."

Damarius started fixing his fro, then began making his stride in their direction. I yanked his tail back.

Angrily I said, "Man, what are you thinkin'? She is here with another dude. We're on a recruiting visit that you weren't even invited to and you're going to cause havoc. Uh, partna, no."

Damarius walked away, frustrated, like I had killed his little Christmas or something. Cole followed him. I stood alone.

The Saxon dude saw me, walked over to me with his girl and said, "You're the big wide out from Georgia, right?" I nodded once. "Well, I'm Saxon Lee. I'm sure you have heard of me. And all the great stuff you've heard can't compare to what I'm really all about."

"You are so full of yourself, Saxon. No wonder your head blows up," the cute girl said real fast.

I liked her. That was her man and she checked him like that in front of me. Dang, not only was she pretty, she was sly. The two of them had words for a second.

Finally, she lifted her hand toward me and said, "Hi, I'm Savoy, his twin sister."

That explains a lot, I thought, as I shook her hand. Her hands felt so soft, I didn't want to let go. *His sister, yes!*

"Let her hand go!" Saxon said as he pulled us apart.

"I'm Perry Skky. Nice to meet you, Savoy," I said as our eyes held.

"Girl, c'mon." Saxon started leading his sister away. "Perry, you better step your game up, brotha. I'ma school you this year. You need to sign quickly. We have a lot of the same college visits and if there is only one wide receiver spot, it's mine."

"Keep runnin' your mouth, Lee. I'ma handle my business on the field," I joked before saying, "And, Miss Savoy, it was very, very nice to meet you. Keep your brother straight."

I didn't see Saxon anymore. We were with different players and hosts and though we were clustered together, we weren't in the same group. I did, however, regret that I didn't see his fine sister again. This campus was expansive and hilly, a nice place, but it was just all right.

They had a new coach, Coach Dan Samson. He used to coach in the SEC and won two national championships with ole Miss. He had gotten an opportunity to coach in the NFL and took it quickly. I think he was making something like three million a year. He was up there for three years and couldn't win worth nothing. Now he was back in college ready to win again. When I was called into his office, while my parents were still seeing the highlight film with my two friends, I didn't really know what to expect.

"Sit down, son, sit down," Coach Samson said as I admired his expansive office.

The chair he sat in almost swallowed him. Looking around and seeing all the awards around him made me so excited that I actually had to take a deep breath. All that I had worked for was real and I was finally being recruited by top schools I'd admired since middle school. But now that it was here, I wasn't all rushed to sign. Yeah, I knew schools were limited on scholarships and to commit early guaranteed I could take a lot of pressure off myself. However, I wanted to check out all my options. I had to stand my ground if he pressured me.

"So, what do you think of USC? It's the best dang school around, huh?" Coach said without waiting on my reply. "Your buddy Cole just committed to come here. We can make it a package deal."

"Well, Coach, I don't know."

"This hesitation, son, is it me? I know a lot of people say that I'm a tough guy to play for. But I bring out the best in my players. Over 60 percent of my squad get hard looks by the NFL and out there 30 percent of my players are still playing today. If that's a level you really want to get to, son, you need to give me a chance. I'm going to be honest with you. Right now we can commit to you, but this is the only time that it is going to be guaranteed. You walk away from South Carolina, we may not be able to offer you a scholarship later."

Coach Samson was laying it on real thick.

"Aw, Coach, I would be honored to play for you. Right now I'm just not sure of where I want to be. I do hope that if I decide to be a Gamecock you'll still have a slot for me. I plan to work hard to keep your interest in me up as I play this year." I stood up to leave, but I shook his hand first.

"I really like you, Skky. We'll stay connected with you through the year. Go have a heck of a football season. Meeting you confirms you're the kind of kid that I want on this team." Before I got out the door, he said softly, "But if you sign with one of my rival schools, I'll make you regret it every year we play you."

We both laughed. I left his office liking him as well. Coach Samson was cool.

As I left the school with my parents and friends, I wondered if I would be back. But it wasn't about me on the ride back, it was about my boy Cole. He had committed to go to college. We went to Golden Corral before getting back on the road and celebrated.

While Cole and my parents went back to the buffet, I noticed Damarius sulking at the table. I knew something was wrong with him. I wanted some more ribs myself, but I sat still.

I asked, "Wasup, dude?"

"Just down, that's all. I'm happy for Cole and I'm even happier for you. I was at your house the other day and saw all your letters from schools. Nobody is knocking at my door for me to play at their school. What I'ma do next year?"

"*This year* you gon' work like you wanna go to college, pull up them grades."

"Boy, please, ain't nobody a bookworm like you."

"How about just opening up the book?"

"Don't even start that," my friend said and looked away.

I said, "Hey, look, man—you can ball on the field. I'm just saying put a little more effort this year in your work, you gon' land somewhere. Watch."

"You think, man?"

I nodded, thinking about all three of us. I just hoped Damarius, Cole and I would really live up to our potential. God was handing us opportunities—why not seize them all?

My other good buddy, Justin Smith, didn't hang with Damarius and Cole. I mean, he wasn't a jock or anything, Justin was a real smart dude. We had AP classes together and though school hadn't started I hadn't seen the brotha in a while, so he came over to show me his new ride.

"It's not as sweet as your two-door new ride," Justin said to me in my driveway as we checked out his shiny black Mustang. "But I won't be walking."

"Man, this is the bomb!" I said.

We went inside for something cold to drink. Summers in Georgia were no joke. My mom never let me down when it came to stocking the refrigerator. I got Justin a cold Gatorade and grabbed another one for myself. Popping off the black top, I gulped that stuff down.

"Dang, boy," Justin said.

"Man, this stuff is an athlete's best friend."

"You know you got it going on right." I gave him a bewildered stare. "I'm just saying, you and I are on two totally different courses."

"What are you talking about?" I asked, wiping my mouth.

"Well, what I'm saying is, you are good-looking. I'm average and sort of small."

"Are you stupid? Talking about I'm cute. You ain't switching up on me, are you?" I teased.

"Real funny. But for real, it ain't like my phone is ringing off the hook."

"You need to get your head up out the books and hang out sometimes."

"What, like I get invited to the cool parties? We hang in class and then when you're with your football crew you don't even give me the time of day."

"Boy, I can't *make* you popular. And I'm never trying to leave you out. Quit putting that all on me."

"I'm just saying let me be around some. It's like this . . . All the cool kids at school are your friends. I want to hang with some of them."

Before we could finish our conversation, my back door was opening. "Knock, knock! It's me and Cole," Damarius yelled.

Cole bear-hugged me and said, "Wasup, homeboy?"

The three of us started rattling on about how we were going to have a great time at our party we were gonna have over at Damarius's house. For a few minutes, I never even turned and acknowledged Justin.

For the first time, I saw what my buddy was saying. He felt like an outsider, and I could do something about it.

"Y'all ain't got no manners," I said to Damarius and Cole. "Y'all see him in here. Speak."

"Hey, Jarred, Jacob, John . . . " Cole said to Justin, then quickly turned to me to get his name.

"His name is Justin. C'mon, y'all, this is my friend and you really need to know him. He could tutor your tails."

"Oh, for real? We need to talk," Damarius said as he slapped Justin's hand. "All right man, you gotta help us throw this party."

Justin smiled at me. Just that quick he was in. I smiled back.

Two days later the party was on. It was filled with honeys and our teammates. We were outnumbered and we loved it. Justin was the only nonathlete male at the party, and he was loving it, too. He got plenty of girls that either thought he was on the team or were just excited to see him with us.

Justin came over to me and said, "See, all you had to do was let me in, bro, and I'll be the man. And, oh, there is this girl named Amandi . . . She wanted me to introduce you to her."

When I turned toward her, my eyes couldn't stop staring at her chest; it was practically completely visible, 'cause she had on a low-cut halter. My gaze eventually moved on to her Daisy Duke shorts. Oh, yeah this party was slammin'!

"So, you gon' dance with me, or what?" Amandi asked as

she moved closer and closer to me, shaking her hips from left to right.

It was easy for me to get in the groove with a girl like that standing in front of me. I wrapped my hands around her waist and let her take me to the middle of the floor. Once I started dancing, everyone joined in. It was crazy. I was now noticing my popularity on a different level. I just hoped God would help me stay humble. I knew I was being tempted.

"You ever seen me before?" she asked, puckering her lips after she said every word, reeling me in with her seductiveness. The girl had it going on, and she had a back like bam! And I was all into it.

"I don't think I know you."

"We're in the same grade at the same school, and you have never noticed me, huh? Well, I'm Amandi Roberts."

"Yeah, didn't you used to wear glasses and braces and—"

"Yeah, and now all that is gone. You like what you see?" she asked as she turned and shook her backside at me. "I wanna be honest, Perry. I wanna . . ." But before she could finish, Damarius and Cole stepped between us and pulled me off the floor.

"What's going on?" I asked the two of them as if they were the chaperone police. "I'm not doing nothing wrong. I'm just having a little fun."

"Yeah, but you about to get us in trouble," Cole said as he hit me in the chest. "Tori is here with Ciara and Briana."

"You broke up with her and you didn't even tell us?" Damarius asked.

They spun me around so that I could look directly at the woman who still had a part of my heart. I hadn't realized it because I tried not to think about it, but the moment I saw her, all the flesh that Amandi was flaunting couldn't hold a candle to the substance I knew Tori possessed. But then I came to my senses. I wasn't trying to go backward, I wanted what Amandi was trying to give away. Tori wasn't about all that and we were through.

I said, "I didn't know I had to answer to the two of you guys. Yeah, I broke up with her."

"Why, dude? Everybody knows that the three of us go with the three of them," Damarius said.

"It's our senior year. If y'all don't wanna be single, which you two need to be because of how bad you cheat on them, anyway, then I'ma show you. You ain't gotta be tied down to be cool."

Damarius replied, "But everybody knows women like a brotha that's already with somebody. If you got game you can play more games."

"Whatever, D. We just think differently."

"All right, do your thing, then, bro."

The two of them backed away and I went back out on the floor to continue dancing with Amandi. When a slow jam came on, I was about to leave. But Amandi didn't let me get too far. She grabbed me back, pulled my body into hers and we rocked with the groove.

"So, what was that about, your boys pulling you away and all?"

"Me and my girl broke up and they just want to make sure I know what I'm doing."

"You looking for another girl?"

"No."

"But you are looking for a good time, right?"

"I don't know." I laughed.

"Well, when that answer is yes, then come to me." She pulled my head close to hers and planted a kiss on me I wasn't expecting.

The crowd did notice and a lot of oohs and ahhs were all around. Quickly, I tried to find Tori in the crowd. I spotted her as she dashed away.

"Uh-uh I gotta go," I said, tugging from Amandi.

It took me a few minutes to find Tori, but when I did she was down the street walking by herself with her hands over her face, crying. The girl cared about me and I knew that. Dang! But she had to get used to us not being together.

I eased up behind her and said, "Hey, hey, hey. Wait a minute."

"Leave me alone, Perry. Just go back in there and get your groove on. Don't let my being upset stop you."

"Wait a minute, babe. Come here." I wiped her tears from her face. "She kissed *me*. I'm not trying to hurt you."

"If you loved me, you would be patient."

I didn't know if what I felt for her was love. We'd been together for a long time, so that should be proof enough to her that I had deep feelings.

"Look, Tori, I do care."

"But you didn't even call me all week."

"I needed some space and plus I had a recruiting visit. I was busy."

"Have you been broken up about us? Have you been missing me? Huh?" Tori pushed.

"Have you changed your mind? Are you willing to do what I want, Tori?" She turned her head and looked away. "Yeah, I'm sorry. It's a tough question for you. But I don't want a no to that question anymore. For us to stay together, on that issue I'm needing a yes."

~ 2 ~

Handling My Business

"**D**ang, boy, you had all day to be ready," my father said as he abruptly came into my room to get me for the Braves baseball game.

I didn't understand why he always had to talk to me any kind of way. I mean, couldn't he have said, "*Son, you ready to go?*" Or something like, "*I'm just coming in here to let you know I'm ready. I'll be downstairs waiting on you.*" Not with my pops. The understanding way he talked to my sister was absent in our conversations, and now he had ticked me off. I had followed him all my life, but suddenly something in me was different now. I wasn't having him come at me incorrectly.

"You in a rush, Pops? Go ahead and go," I said as I sat on my bed. I started taking off my hoodie. "I'm sure somebody at the dealership wouldn't mind going in my place."

"Boy, put that daggone shoe on and get your tail up so we can go! I'm rushing you because I gotta pick up Mr. Graham and Dakari, and I'm trying not to hold them up and be late 'cause of you. Now let's go!"

My dad could still make me do some things, but I didn't have to like it. I didn't know company was riding with us. Actually, that was going to make the journey to Atlanta much better for me. I hadn't seen Dakari in a good while. He was my sister's old high school boyfriend. Their on-and-off relationship was a trip! He wanted to play the field. Thankfully, my sister caught on.

I'll never forget the day Dakari and I almost got to fighting. I'd admired him for so long, but when he embarrassed my sister in public by breaking up with her in front of a big crowd at school, I stood up to him. I had to be a man. I had to let him know that when it came to my sister, I wasn't having it. We didn't actually come to blows, though. But ever since that day, Dakari has been givin' me my props. He told me that he knew I had fire that would take me far.

I didn't know how this little father-son trip of my dad's would go. The Grahams had just gone through a serious tragedy. Their oldest son, Drake, who was the starting linebacker for the Atlanta Falcons, got gunned down at a club in Athens. Dakari actually saw the whole thing. And from what my sister said, the brotha was still sorta messed up from it all.

I didn't talk to God as much as I needed to, but as we pulled into their driveway and my dad honked the horn, I silently talked to the Lord. *"Oh, Lord. What am I supposed to say to these people? They gotta be hurt still. Not only was Drake a superstar around here, but he was family to them. How do you get over such pain? How, as a friend, can I say anything that will lift them up? Be with us in this car and even with me and my dad, because You know he's trying my patience."*

Actually, the ride down was real cool. Mr. Graham was laughing with my dad about this and that. Dakari was joking about crazy college life. It wasn't until the conversation turned toward me that things got uncomfortable. Dakari had to ask the question that made my dad rattle off at the mouth. I hated that my father thought he knew what was best for me and that his decisions were the only ones that needed to be followed.

Dakari said, "So, man, where you gon' play college ball? I know those schools coming at you from every direction!"

"Yeah, Junior, who you gon' sign with?" Mr. Graham asked me from the front seat.

"Aww, man, you know that boy don't know," my father cut in as if I was some baby not knowing my way home from nursery school.

Shoot, I was practically a grown man! I'm 'bout to be out the crib, and he tryin' to act. If I wanted to, I could get on MapQuest and find directions to any college I wanted to make a recruiting visit to. I could stroll into Duke, UGA or Miami solo. My pops wasn't as needed as he thought he was, but I just let him ramble on.

I looked at Dakari and said, "I narrowed it down to six schools."

"Georgia's one of them, right?" Dakari chimed in as if he'd be happy to have me on his team again.

We slapped hands, sorta feeling each other. Boy, he was cool. I was glad he still thought I was.

"I wouldn't mind him going up there so his sister could keep an eye on him and you too, Dakari," my dad said, still thinking of me as incapable of standing on my own. "But his mom is thinking of a more academic school."

"Football and academics?" Dakari asked with a laugh. "You still gettin' all them A's without trying?"

"Lay off him now, Dakari. There is nothing wrong with a smart guy that can ball," Mr. Graham said as he turned and looked at me. "That's good, man. Keep it up. Many of these young brothers got talent on the football field, but ain't got nothing upstairs. If they're fortunate enough to get in college, for most they can't even keep up their grades to stay in there. There is enough pressure to worry about as a college athlete without grades coming into play. You'll pick the right school."

"Oh, yeah. I'm going to help him and make sure he does that," my dad once again responded. I looked out the window, hating that I was resenting him.

At the game, Dakari and I walked to get some snacks. "Ooh, Atlanta is nice!" I said as the lights I saw from downtown impressed me.

"Oh, no! Don't tell me you're thinking about Georgia Tech?" Dakari joked, as he punched me in the arm. "We'll go from high school teammates to college rivals in a hurry, buddy! But yo smart tail, I should've known that's where you was thinking 'bout going!"

"Naw, naw, I ain't made no decisions. I mean, I'ma go down to visit, but I never saw myself as an engineer."

Dakari touched my shoulder. "For real, though, I sensed you and your dad are not on the same page. You wanna talk about it?"

"Naw, I'm straight," I said, knowing that I wasn't, but didn't wanna burden Dakari with anything since the brotha was still grieving. "I don't need to stress you out with my stuff, man."

We ordered eight hot dogs, four nachos, four large drinks and two candy bars. "Naw, man, you ain't gon' burden me. I wouldn't have asked you if I didn't wanna offer help. I understand crazy daddies, trust me. Mine's fronting, or maybe he's just turning the corner. He hasn't really spoken to me since my brother's been gone. I don't know if he blames me that I couldn't do more to save Drake, or if he secretly wishes that I would've been the one dead instead."

"Man, don't say that." I hated hearing Dakari talk that way.

He was just expressing his feelings, and I didn't even ask if I could help. I knew I had to say something so he wouldn't think so negatively. Maybe the Lord would answer my prayers and help me say the right things to Dakari!

Feeling words pour out of my heart, I said, "Grief is a hard thing to get over, man. Remember, my grandfather died around the same time as your brother did. Even though he was older than all of us, we still didn't want him to go. Just imagine, your dad probably never thought about burying his son. And I'm sure that his losing Drake has nothing to do with loving you less. He's probably making sure he can love you right."

Drake chuckled. "All right, I hear you, man. Don't get all emotional on me, now. What's up with you and your dad?"

I went on to explain to Dakari that my father always thought he had all the answers. I also told him that my dad still treated me like a little boy. I admitted that my dad got on my nerves when he acted like that.

As we walked back to our seats, Dakari said, "Let me tell you like this, even though you think you know everything, which you probably know more than what your dad is giving you credit for, just try not to shut him out. You gotta take him on recruiting visits. I seen the brothers who go with no dads and they get treated differently. The ones that go with concerned parents really get special treatment from the coaches and stuff. It seems crazy, but at least they know you have other options and a family that will help you make it without football. For the folks that come in there with nobody, the coaches do a half-spill! I'm not saying that your dad has to choose the college for you, but he should be a part of this. Some of those college coaches—trust me, all right? Find a way to tolerate your dad because you'll need him around. He can help you keep everything straight."

I was going to have to remember what Dakari said. Maybe my dad could still hang with me some. However, it was what it was and if the relationship was going to get better, God was the only one that could do it. I wasn't going to be no punk and kiss his behind. I did love him, though, and that had to count for something.

* * *

The next day, I was ready to go shoot some hoops with my boys when my sister and Tad practically begged me to go with them on a double date.

"Please say you'll go!" Payton said. "When I was in high school, I used to do so many favors for you. When you couldn't drive, I'd take you anywhere you wanted to go."

"A double date? I ain't trying to get serious with nobody, Pay."

Tad Taylor, my sister's boyfriend of two years, cut in and said, "Oh, trust me, partner, it's my cousin and I don't want her serious with nobody right now. Actually, that's why I wanna introduce her to you. You know, show her some other options. This one dude she likes, I'm not feeling him."

"What you mean?" I probed.

My sister looked at me with a smirk on her face, pointed to her skin and shook her head. "Not brown."

"Your cousin is dating a white boy?" I got very interested and asked, "She ugly, huh? The brothers don't want her?"

"No, she ain't ugly, Perry. She is cute, for real. She doesn't want the brothers."

"Where we going?" I asked, down to find out what kind of black girl wasn't into the brothas.

"We'll go eat, maybe play Putt-Putt, or head to the park or something. So, you can keep on what you have on," my sister said.

"Cool. I'll meet up with my boys tomorrow, then. How are you gon' get her to meet up with me if she don't like black guys?" I inquired.

Tad replied, "She thinks she is just gonna meet my girlfriend and hang out with us. So, you down with surprising her, or what?"

"I ain't trying to be conceited or nothing, but as long as

y'all know I'm not trying to be serious. Girls get hooked on me quick!"

"Oh, I see you done grown up," Tad teased. "Trust me. If anything, you'll be into her."

I joked, "What? . . . All right. I got to meet her, then."

Later, as we left Augusta and went to Aiken, South Carolina, out in the country, I started having second thoughts. *What was I doing going a blind date, anyways?* I still had feelings for Tori. Yeah, I was trying to be all hard and suppress them, act like I didn't care and all, but I did. I shook it off by telling myself, *It's not gonna matter, I'm just going out. Besides, me and Tori are over. I need to move on.*

What if this chick is ugly and I can't even look at her for five minutes? That'll be wack. I can do this. Plus, I know my sister wouldn't set me up with no ugly girl. Payton loves the world of style; she's got that eye for fashion and stuff. If she says a girl is cute, then I can trust that.

I couldn't believe the chick lived off a dirt road. I ain't ever been to Tad's house, but Payton told me he lived in a trailer. I mean, there ain't nothing wrong with that, but let me say that I'm just happy we wasn't in my ride. Just then we turned down a long street that led to a gorgeous house set off by itself on a whole bunch of acres of land.

"Dang!" I commented from the back.

Tad said, "Yeah, my uncle got bread! He was some high vp at the Savannah River Plant. I hope my crazy cousin ain't home," Tad said before getting out of the passenger side.

"Why you say that? I thought we were here to pick up your cousin? Don't be leaving me out here in these boonies to wait for her!" I replied.

"No, no, he meant his boy-cousin. She has a twin brother that is full of himself," my sister said. She went on to tell me that she was surprised I hadn't met the guy, being that he was highly recruited just like me.

Before I could think through the A-list of South Carolina players, a familiar-looking girl began walking back to the car with Tad. Out of my mouth came the name. "Savoy!"

"You know her?" my sister turned and asked me.

"Sorta. I know her crazy brother, too. I'm glad he ain't here. If he knew I was taking out his sister, he probably would've come out here with the shotgun even though I'm with his cousin!"

Tad opened the door and said, "Savoy, this is Payton's brother, Perry. Perry, meet my cousin, Savoy."

"Oh, my gosh, it's you!" she said with a smile as she happily got in the car.

The girl was fine with a capital *F*! I didn't know how to guess sizes, but she sure had the best of everything. Curves in the right places, jet-black hair flowing halfway down her back. She had a cute style going on, too—Savoy was rockin' with stilettos, jeans and a pink Baby Phat shirt. She was classy with it. Yeah, definitely a classy girl. Savoy had the prettiest sun-kissed brown skin, lookin' like honey-coated chocolate!

If Damarius was with me, he'd be all over her. Tad also introduced her to my sister. After the formalities, we drove back into town.

"What's up, lady?" I asked in a cool voice.

"Y'all know each other?" Tad asked, all confused.

My sister explained, "Apparently, it's Perry and Saxon who know each other. They were just at the University of South Carolina together."

"I went on the trip, too," Savoy said, "and I got to meet this guy here!"

She nudged me in the arm, and I liked her touch. She wasn't coming on to me, and she wasn't shy, either. I couldn't figure it out, but I was intrigued.

"Well, we gon' talk up here and y'all can talk back there," Tad said.

After a few moments of awkwardness, I began, "Savoy, I'm sorry we threw a blind date on you, but your cousin made me."

"I wasn't okay with it when he told me as we were walking to the door, but I can deal with it now," she said as she looked me up and down.

Dinner at Chili's was a lot of fun. The conversation was light. We didn't talk about football. We didn't talk about school. We didn't even talk about the white boy. Actually, Payton and Tad dominated most of the conversation, filling us in on college life.

The chemistry between my sister and her boyfriend was cool. Dakari was always my pick for her, but he tripped. Though I didn't know how long this thing with Tad would last, I was for it. He was so into God. I really admired that. I wished I was there, but I knew in my heart that some distance had come between God and I over the last couple of years. Tad was a role model for me more than he knew. As a college running back at Georgia, he could have any girl. However, I couldn't imagine him doing Payton wrong. I liked him.

His eyes showed my sister meant the world to him. Knowing she had someone at college that really cared for her left me off the hook with the thought of attending University of Georgia. In the back of my mind, over the last year and a half, I knew I wanted to be up there just to make sure she was all right.

I had gone to the same school with my sister all my life. Dakari, too, for that matter. Going to a different college from them would give me the chance to step out of their shadow and have my own light going on. The thought of not being anybody's little brother and making my own mark was real appealing.

As we played a game of Putt-Putt behind Tad and Payton, Savoy and I started talking about that very thing.

"I know it has to be stressful for you. All those schools wanting you, and hoping you make the right decision. My brother won't admit it, but he's terrified of choosing the wrong one. Why does Saxon have to be so cocky? He's got the skills, but why flaunt like that?"

Trying to gain brownie points, I said, "I don't know. He's your brother, so I want to say he can't be all that bad. But the brief few times we'd talked . . . I admit he is crazy!"

"I know, I know. I guess the saying 'You can't live with him, can't live without him' definitely applies to how I feel about my brother. He didn't actually start becoming all great until recently. My parents, well, really, my dad, who's sorta like a father to Tad, were getting close. When Saxon started to see that, he applied his attention to football, and diverted my dad's attention back to where he wanted. I don't know why my brother's like that. We get everything we need, so we should be secure. We only moved to the country so my dad could be close to his mom, who lives in a sweet little house you passed before you got to our house."

"Oh, yeah, I remember."

As we came to the eleventh hole, I knew I wanted to talk deep with Savoy. She'd asked me about my world. We'd talked about football and her brother and all that, but I had some questions of my own.

"What is it that you want to ask me? You keep staring and nothing is coming out your mouth. What? Tad wanted you to meet me because he hates my boyfriend, right?"

"Maybe."

"Oh, yeah, I know that's the reason. That's the only thing he and Saxon have in common besides football."

"So, is it that you like this particular white boy, or you just like white boys, period? I just gotta know 'cause I never heard of such a thing if the latter is true."

Savoy said, "Well, the latter is true in this case, okay? I'm through with brothas. My cousin Tad is a rare exception. He loves Jesus way too much to mess up. And now that he's so in love with your sister, he definitely ain't gon' mess up! But that is the complete opposite with my brother. He has ten black books full of numbers and he can't even keep girls' names straight! And his friends, the pack he runs with, they are all dogs. They show no respect, and they're full of bad intentions. I'm tired of dealing with it, so I choose not to."

If she was saying all black guys were bad, I couldn't agree with that. Yeah, some of us didn't treat girls the best. Some of us did, though. My face reflected my disagreement.

She continued, "And don't be looking at me like I'm full of it, 'cause I'm sure your boys are the same way. I met them in Columbia, remember. Most black guys have no respect for girls, not even trying to court and go the extra mile to keep us happy. So, if a white boy is what it takes, then a white boy is what I'll get. Now, don't hate me because I said that. If a blonde-haired, blue-eyed doll was flinging her hair at you, trust me, you'll take the bait and forget all about the sisters, too. You don't seem to be as crazy as my brother. I know you don't have just one girlfriend. What do you have, about five?"

"Now, why would you think that of me? Actually, I had a girlfriend. I don't know if you could say that I was a Tad, because Tad ain't trying to have no sex. That's why me and my girl broke up. In reality, I got needs, you know? But I was faithful to her. I still care about her. Even though it's time for me to move on, that doesn't mean I'm gon' be a dog."

"But listen to what you're saying . . . There's somebody that you still care for and yet you're not willing to fight for her. Ugh! Brothers don't wanna work at a relationship. And because there are so many women that outnumber y'all, you guys get to play it like that. I just don't respect that way of thinking."

"You can't respect me?" I asked. "I am disappointed that you can't understand where I was coming from."

"I'm not judging you, Perry. I mean, you're a cool guy. But how can I be feeling like you're the world's greatest when you had this girl, and she wasn't giving it up when you wanted, so you just bailed? It's like you don't care about her feelings enough to wait. Do you think that's right?"

I couldn't answer her. She had me stumped on that one. She was giving me a lot to think about. Was I taking care of things the right way in my life when it came to Tori? I mean, I did miss the girl. I was all confused, but I knew soon I would get it figured out.

I put that conversation to the side and enjoyed the rest of the time I had with the sassy girl I liked talking to. Hanging out with Savoy, I knew I couldn't do anything right then about Tori, so there was no need stressing about that. I liked the point where I was. I was a man. I wasn't a dog, but I was a brother who definitely knew what I liked. And I couldn't say that was all bad.

"Come on, Damarius, man. You slippin'. You can't press two hundred? What's up?" I teased my boy as we lifted weights.

Damarius tried again. "Aw, Perry, lay off me. I'm handling mines. I got this. You just step back and get on out the way."

"Cole, you better get over there and spot the boy before he falls out! You know that's still too much for him," I taunted as Cole nodded.

Actually, I knew Damarius really could lift the weight, but sometimes he thought he couldn't. I had to trick him. Use negative reinforcement to get him to cross over the line. If he wanted to show me up to make me think he was the man, then he'd do it. And that's just what he did.

"Take that! I should've bet you, man. I would've been rich," Damarius said as soon as he put the weights back on the bar.

He and Cole slapped hands, and I nodded my head in approval. If he could get those grades up, then all three of us would be going to college for sure. I just hated that it seemed I had more dreams for my friend than he had for himself. I couldn't understand why that was, but I couldn't give up on him. I cared about his crazy self too much.

Next, it was Cole's turn. He was loading a lot more weight to both ends of the bar.

Damarius got up in my face and said, "Hey, man, why you stand us up yesterday, anyways?"

"I ain't stand y'all up," I responded. "I called and left a message on both of y'all cell phones."

"You ain't tell us what you had to do," Damarius fronted me.

"I had a date." I said. "Come on, Cole. Man, don't listen to him. Do your thing. I gotta bench press, too."

Cole didn't move. He was waiting on me to elaborate, while Damarius sat on the other side of the bench also waiting on me to tell them my business. At first I was hesitant. Discussing it with them would only lead to the "S" question. But then I realized they knew this girl, and it would be interesting to get their take on the whole thing.

"You know my sister's boyfriend, right?"

"Some dude from Aiken," Cole said. "He plays with Dakari at Georgia."

"Yeah. I went out with his cousin," I responded.

"Dang! You had a blind date. They set you up? Was she tore up, bro?" Damarius asked, laughing.

I bragged, "Man, you would've wanted to be in my shoes last night. Trust me."

Damarius boasted back. "Please. Ciara keeps me busy enough and plus, I gotta whole bunch of extras on the side that I'm quite satisfied with, thank ya kindly. I don't want Perry Skky's leftovers."

"Not even if it's that girl we met at USC with her twin brother, Saxon?"

"You ain't go out with her," Damarius said, coming over to my side of the bar.

"For real, you did?" Cole responded, as he saw in my face that I was serious.

"What? So Saxon is related to your sister's boyfriend?" Damarius asked.

"Yeah, they're first cousins. I didn't even see him, but his sister was straight."

"Man, we trying to get you hooked back up with Tori!" Cole said.

"Actually, Savoy was talking that same stuff last night," I revealed. They both looked at me as if I'd spoken Chinese.

"So, you saying you went out with a new girl that's telling you to get back with your old girl? You're losing your touch, Perry. You need to step aside and give me her number!" Damarius said, trippin' like he was the man.

I busted his bubble and told him, "You the wrong color, homeboy."

"Oh, she likes them white boys?" Cole asked. And I nodded. "As dark as you is Damarius, you far from her taste!"

"Man, she probably was with that wrong kinda dark chocolate that ain't have no taste. But wait til she have a piece of this sweet stuff! I'll win her back over to the brothers, trust me. The digits, please," my friend said as he held out his hand before I tapped it and pushed it aside.

I said, "Come on, Cole. Finish the workout."

"For real, though, if she already taken—white, black, Boricua, it don't matter—you need to do what you gotta do and listen to her or us and get back with Tori. Brianna told me the girl been crying," Cole said as he laid down to bench press.

I hit him on the head. We finished our brutal workout. Before we parted ways, they made me promise I'd think about the whole Tori thing.

Later that night as I tried thinking about football and school, I sat on the couch and all I could do was think about Tori. I didn't need any persuading. I missed being with the girl. I missed seeing her cute little face. I missed hearing her sweet, precious voice. What had I done breaking it off?

My mom brought me a plate of food. It was actually a bowl of food, a little country shrimp boil with crab legs, corn on the cob, potatoes, sausage and shrimp all smothered together in a broth. Dang, it looked good! I didn't know where to start. I was still so messed up with my heartbreak that I brought on heartburn and couldn't eat it. I sat it on the coffee table, and my mom sat next to me.

"Okay, something's wrong with you. My son not eating? What's up?"

"Naw, Mom. I'm straight."

I was a big boy. I didn't need my mom all in my problems. Plus, I didn't want her knowing that I just wanted to have sex. Naw, that was okay.

"Did I tell you Tori called?"

Quickly my head turned toward her. "No, when?"

"She actually called a couple of times, but I spoke to her the last time she called. She sounded sorta down, too."

"What'd she say?"

"Mmmm, just that you weren't too happy with her, and that she thought you guys were over for good this time. Is that true, Son?"

"Oh, come on, Mom!"

"Oh, come on, Junior! You're my son. I'm a woman. Looks like you got troubles with your girlfriend. Talk to me."

"Trust me, just take her side."

"Is her side the right one? The one that would honor God?"

"Where'd that come from, Mom? Dang!"

" 'Cause, boy, I raised you to know what's right from wrong. And if what she's standing for will please God, then you need to quit tripping, cut her some slack and get over your own selfish ways. How about that? You don't have to tell me nothing. We don't have to talk about it. You don't even have to eat my food. But I know you ain't crazy, and I know you're hungry. You'll ponder on what I said, and you'll eat all this in front of you," she said.

She was right, too. I was making myself sick over my decision to cut things off with Tori. I only hoped I could figure out what was right to do. Mom's grub was smellin' good. I felt my appetite coming back.

She continued, "I worry about you a lot. You're about to go out into the real world. I know you're more than just book-smart. You're street-smart, too. So, use your common sense, 'cause you ain't no fool. I never wanted you to get too serious with girls. Thankfully, the one you got has her head on straight. It's a whole bunch of these fast mamas out here that I certainly don't want you to get caught all up with. So, if you're with Tori, at least Mom won't have to stress, you know? Plus the girl truly cares for you, she's not around for the sport, not around for the fame. Think about that, Son."

She kissed me on my forehead and left me to my thoughts. I kept looking at the phone beside me, picked it up and dialed Tori's number that was etched in my brain. When I got her answering machine, I left a message telling her how I really felt.

"My mom told me you called. I don't know. If an apology is enough for you to forgive me, then I'm sorry I've been pushing you away. Even though I've physically kept my distance, you haven't been out of my heart and mind. I want us to get back together. If that's what you want, then give me a call. I miss you, girl."

After I hung up the phone, I picked up the seafood dish in front of me and gobbled it down. My mom was right. I wasn't crazy. Tori was a great girl and the food was the bomb! All I could do was my part. I didn't know if she would take me back. I just knew I wanted her to. And now the ball was in her court.

Until she called me, I had to relax. Lay off it a bit. Though I made some mistakes with her, I had made my bed, and now I had to sleep in it. If she didn't take me back, I'd find a way to be cool with it. I was tough, but I also knew when to admit when I was wrong. For the first time in a long time I could feel good, knowing that with my girlfriend I was handling my business.

~ 3 ~

Being in Control

I became more filled with excitement with each mile I drove to Lucy Laney High School. It was time to get ready for the first day of football camp. This was my senior year. Though I was one of the top recruits in the state going into football season, I was ready to try and be the best player in Georgia. Not because I had something to prove to anyone else, but I wanted to prove to myself that I was great at the game I'd worked so hard on. For so many years, I'd studied the game, watched the film and learned from coaches. Now I was ready to perform.

I also knew this wasn't going to be a cakewalk, either. As many fans as I had out there, I had many naysayers who were wanting me to fail, wanting me to give up and not wanting me to live up to my expectations. And all of that just made me strive harder and become more explosive on the field.

When I pulled up to the parking lot, everybody on my team was pulling up at the same time. Looked like they were as eager as I was. We were ready to win state and take it to the Dome. Show people some things. Show them that this little school from Augusta was a powerhouse. There was one big setback, though. And that was the fact that we had a new head coach. Coach Pugh, our former leader, had come upon a great opportunity. He had wanted to coach on a college level for years. He now was the head coach for Fort Valley State University, a historically black college in Fort Valley, Georgia, about three hours away from us.

Some young guy named Coach Robinson, who had won a national college championship at Georgia Tech in 1990, was our new coach. He had played a couple of years with some pro team. I didn't know much about him, but I heard he was a pretty cocky guy. Though I had been in the school's weight room a lot over the summer, our paths had never crossed. He'd invited me to his home for dinner, and had other team member meetings, but I missed them due to my trip to South Carolina and family vacations.

I got called into the coach's office before I could even put on my pads. I wondered, *What does he want with me right now?*

"Perry Skky! I'm excited that you could honor me with your presence," Coach Robinson said sarcastically.

I sat down in a chair and said, "All right, Coach. You gotta problem with me or somethin'?"

I wanted to have respect for the man, but he didn't need to come at me like I was a chump player. The respect thing was a two-way street, and he needed to know that up front. I wasn't asking for first-class treatment, but he wasn't about to make me redeem my stripes again, either.

He stood up from behind his desk. He was a buff dude. He came on around, looked me straight in the eyes and boldly said, "I understand that you can be a flash player. A lot of colleges think you got unbelievable talent. 'Throw the ball to Perry. He can make amazing things happen!' papers say. Well, on my offense, I call the plays. If I want you to get the ball, then, and only then, will you have it. I don't like show-

offs. I'm the coach here and I run the show, you understand?"

"Never questioned it. Is that all?"

What did he expect me to do? Get down on my hands and
knees and worship him or somethin'? Yeah, right. He could
talk all that lame stuff. I'd show him out there on the field
that the team really did respect me.

Almost reading my mind he said, "In order to be a leader,
Perry, you gotta have the respect of your teammates."

"I do, Coach."

"I don't think so. Marlon Barksdale was in here all summer going on and on about how you think the game is all
about you."

"He's just hating."

I mean, that was a joke to me. Marlon was on the other
side of the field with my same position. He was just jealous
that the ball mostly came to me. When he did get the ball
into his hands, he let the team down, missing catch after
catch.

In reality, he couldn't keep up with me on any level. Academically, he wasn't on the Principal's List, making straight A's.
Socially, none of the girls were after him. He really had it out
for me because my girl was the one he had wanted so desperately. She wouldn't give him the time of day. Economi-
cally, his car looked like a broke-down Beetle, which could
barely make it from point A to point B. And physically, he had
nothing on me. He was a short receiver with sloppy hands,
and he wasn't as quick as he needed to be.

Of course the guy was going to down me. Marlon couldn't
beat me, and I didn't want him to join me. He was stupid and
made dumb decisions. And in his mind, all he wanted to do
was bring me down. But if the coach wanted to get on his
bandwagon, fine with me.

"Whatever, Coach. I don't have the respect of the team, 'cause you listen to Barksdale. All right, cool."

"Well, you seem a little arrogant with me right now. Why should I think that you're a humble guy?"

"Coach, you're getting on me, and I don't even know you!"

"So, why don't you make me wanna like you? Why are you making it so difficult?"

"I give off what I get, sir. Not trying to be difficult, just being real. I won't give you any problems on the field. If you wanna give me the ball, it's your call. Is that all, Coach?"

"For now, Perry. That's all."

I was so sorry in practice that first day. For the second and third day, I wasn't at full speed, either. Neither was the rest of the team. I wasn't showing any leadership. I wasn't trying to motivate them or correct them. Coach Robinson thought he was the man, and he needed to step up and clear up the mess that I was seeing before me.

At lunch, Cole came up to me and we sat down under a tree. We nibbled on ham sandwiches and chips, and drank Gatorade. Then I caught my boy looking at me like I'd let him down.

"Perry, what's with you? We better do something. We got a game next weekend. If we keep playing the way we practicing, we're gonna get beat like we stole something!"

"Why you over here talking to me about it? I ain't the head coach. Go talk that mess to him," I said as I pointed to Coach Robinson.

"He coaches offense. That's why I'm talking to you. Shoot, the defense is tight! Y'all ain't score nothing on us, even in the scrimmage yesterday. Coach said something to you the first day, and you still trippin'. But let me ask you this. You gon' let him stop what's inside of you to do?"

"What you talking 'bout, Cole?"

"I'm just saying, Perry, you're a leader. And you're being suppressed because of what somebody said to you. Coach Robinson ain't nobody. Don't let him ruin what's yours this season. Every team needs a leader. And you the man. Be it."

"I couldn't have said it better myself, Cole," Coach Robinson replied from behind us.

Cole was startled. "Oh, Coach, Coach, Coach, Coach!"

My friend had his foot caught in his mouth, talking about our head coach and he was listening. I didn't care, though. I was glad the man heard that other players thought he wasn't all that.

"Give me ten laps while I talk to your boy," he told Cole.

I questioned, "You gon' make him run laps because you stepped in on our private conversation?"

"I'm making him run 'cause he looked a little slow out there in practice today. But you and I need to talk. Go 'head, Cole," Coach Robinson said. My friend quickly jogged away.

"You think I don't like you, huh?" Coach asked.

"I know you don't like me."

"And that makes you real angry, like you don't wanna put forth no effort, right? Like you're trying to punish me and do bad."

"I ain't trying to punish nobody, I'ma do mine. You give the ball to me. I'll make something happen with it. If you don't, then the rest of the world will know that your play calling is definitely questionable."

"So, as I said to you earlier in the week, it is about you, isn't it?"

"It's really not about me, Coach, is it? You're the leader. This is yo thang. How come you're not able to get the team looking any better?"

"I played on the highest level, Perry, and it's not easy up there. I know you're a smart kid, but to be great at anything in life, you gotta overcome obstacles. Even ones that are self-imposed."

I didn't know what he was talking about then. But for the first time, it didn't seem like he was talking *at* me but talking *to* me. And for that, I kept listening.

"I said some tough things to you 'cause I wanted you to step up and be a leader. But you stepped back. Instead of letting what I said challenge you, you let it take the air and wind outta your sail."

Was he right? Did I let him make me less of who I was?

"In reality, Perry, I am the one who calls the plays and makes the decisions. But this team needs both of us to succeed. You are a senior and you are a captain. Don't be passive. Do your job. Don't let any situation or anybody make you abandon it. Not even me. You're over here eating with only one player, while the rest of your team is over there trying to get a spark going. What are you going to do about it? We have a game in a week. I don't know if you want the NFL, but I know you want the state championship. I had a talk with Coach Pugh, and he told me you wanted it. So, what are you going to do to get it? What are you going to do to help your teammates get it?"

When the coach patted me on the back and took off, catching up with Cole to jog with him, I realized something. Though I didn't agree with his methods, maybe his methods were what I needed to take my game to another level. I cleaned up my mess, headed over to the team and gave a speech while Coach and Cole were jogging.

"If we wanna win state, we gotta win in practice. I'ma let it start with me. I'm taking my effort up another notch. Y'all with me or not?"

The guys started cheering and roaring.

Damarius got in front of me, chanting, "Number 1! Number 1!"

The whole team started saying it, and I started believing it. I didn't have to be in control of the team for me to do my part. If we all just worked to our highest level possible, big things could happen.

We got out there and practice was on point! Coach said nothing to me when it was over, but he did smile my way. Then I realized I was glad he was here.

"Daaang, man. Hand me a tissue. I'm all emotional," Damarius joked as we walked into the building on the first day of school.

"Boy, you stupid!" I said and laughed back with him.

I couldn't believe it, either. The first day of my senior year. Wow! I wasn't overly emotional or sentimental, but I was feeling a little something.

I actually had a bruised ego, 'cause I hadn't heard back from Tori since I left her a message about wanting to reconcile. I didn't know what was up with that. Why she couldn't give a brother another chance? But I knew when she first saw me she wouldn't be able to ignore what was on both of our hearts.

Cole came up behind us and said, "Perry, man, what's up? You losing your touch or something?"

"What you talking 'bout, man?" I replied.

"Check out your girl and your favorite teammate."

I couldn't believe Tori was walking hand in hand with Marlon Barksdale.

"Hold my stuff," I said to Damarius.

"Man, you ain't going over there. Chill out!" Cole said.

"Naw, naw, he need to go over there and get Tori back. He can't let no underclassman take his girl," Damarius said as he walked behind me.

As if I still had some claim to her, I said, "Tori, what's up with this? Why you holding this joker's hand?"

"That's a dumb question, Skky. Why you think?" Marlon mouthed off as he took two steps torward my face.

"Ooh, I'm shaking."

I pushed him back lightly, and the soft shove pushed him into the crowd. Folks started laughing, but he wasn't on my mind right then. I looked at Tori, grabbed her chin, tilted her head toward mine and said, "What you doing? You don't want us anymore?"

Before she could respond, Marlon stepped back in my face. "Okay, man, wait. What you tryin' to do?"

"Can't you see I'm standing here talking to my girl?" I asked.

"Yo girl?" Marlon asked. "She was with me last night. Tori, you might as well go on and tell him. We're all the way together. You know what I mean. I've been to places with her you only wished you could go."

I snapped. "Tori, what is he talking 'bout?"

I knew Marlon wasn't talking about sex. I knew there was no way in the world that my girl would give it up to him! Or anybody. Particularly since she wasn't letting me have my way. Had my breaking up with her caused her to lose her mind? Naw.

Why was she acting like this? She wasn't denying it. She wasn't saying, *"Why you lying on me?"* She was taking it. She wasn't showing any emotion. Just looking at me with those sad, puppy-dog eyes. What was I supposed to make of that? What was I supposed to assume?

"If it's like that, then fine," I finally responded to both of them.

"Yeah, it's like that, and it's *real* good," Marlon mouthed off.

Tori dashed away. I wasn't gonna follow her, either. Had she really given herself to someone other than me? I couldn't even bear the thought of it. And to Marlon Barksdale? I would never fully appreciate her for who she was anymore. His tail was a wannabe. Just wannabe somebody he wasn't. On the serious tip, everyone knew he wanted to be me.

We stood looking at each other too hard, like if anybody said anything it was on. My boys pulled me away. That joker had the nerve to talk smack.

"Yeah, you better go."

Wrestling with my boys I said, "D, y'all need to let me go. Cole, you need to let go of my arm so I can take care of this dude. I'm sick of him running his mouth."

"Naw, man, it ain't even worth it," Damarius said. "You need to go on to them accelerator classes you taking."

Cole laughed and said, "It's accelerated classes, fool."

Nothing was funny to me. However, they did have a point. My schedule was really brutal. I was on the college prep track. Just looking at the syllabus for each of my classes should've freaked me out! I would have tons of papers to write, a lot of tests to take, plenty of research to do. But I didn't care, I just had to do what I had to do to move on. Right now, I cared 'bout Tori.

As I strolled to class, the crowds assured me that my popularity status was still intact. It really made my ego feel good when girls came up to me giving me their numbers. Or when guys wanted to hold a conversation with me about the upcoming game, telling me I was going to do great. Even though my girl had chosen another dude on the first day of school, I was still the man. I had girls lining up to take her place. And the reason why guys were wanting my time was so they could raise their own status. I guess I should've been happy, but that really didn't matter. All I could think about was what Tori was doing to me.

Just then Justin came by. We had all the same classes. He was still popular from being at the big party before school started.

"Man, I don't know what you're stressing about that girl for," he said. "It's not like you're losing anything. You broke up with her, anyway. I ain't trying to bring you down or nothing, but isn't this what you wanted? Her to move on?"

"I didn't want her giving it up to anybody other than me, though. You know?"

"So, it is not that she was with Marlon this morning, but that she was *really, really* with Marlon that gets you?"

"All of it, I guess. I just want her back. I mean, I did before I knew how far she'd gone with him."

"So, you see her as dirty now?" Justin asked honestly.

"I don't know," I yelled. "I'm trying to figure it all out."

When school was over, Justin went up to the office. He was student body president, and had some meeting to attend. I went on to the locker room. He hadn't given me any advice, but he did call me out, made me think about what I was feeling. Though I had no intention of putting all of that into perspective, I was boiling. Shoot, I was ticked off!

When Marlon was the first face I saw in the locker room, I snapped. I rushed up to him, grabbed him by the collar, pinned him up against his locker and abruptly said, "You a lie, chump! You ain't never have that!"

"You just mad 'cause you never had it. Not like we can compare notes," Marlon taunted.

I let him go. I wasn't 'bout to fight him over no girl. He grabbed me by my neck and pulled out a scrawny pocket-knife.

"What's that supposed to do, scare me?" I asked.

As he clenched my neck tighter and tighter, I could hardly speak because his grip had me. He dug the point of the knife in the corner of my eye.

"Don't charge at me again, Skky, or embarrass me in front of the whole school. So, whether you and your girl ever get down or not, it doesn't matter. By the time I'm done getting it so good, there won't be nothing left for you to enjoy."

With that I kicked him in the knee. The knife slid and cut me. That's when Coach Robinson came in. That was good, 'cause ain't no telling what I would've done to that chump.

"Skky, go see the trainer. Barksdale, you're suspended off this team for Friday's game. I'm not tolerating any team member using weapons. And, boy, what the heck were you thinking?" he asked as he hit him on the back of his head.

I got to sit practice out. The cut on my eye felt deep. Coach wanted to see me in his office again when he saw I looked in pain. Trying to be tough, I told him I was okay.

He said, "I'm really surprised at you. I gave you the chance at being a leader, and you're fighting your teammate over some girl."

"I wasn't fighting him."

"And the second time today. I hear y'all had it out earlier in the hallway. You got too bright of a future to be putting it all on the line for some girl."

"He was lying on her, Coach. What was I supposed to do, just let him bash her name?"

"Come on, man. The girl knows what she's doing. She was just trying to get a rise outta you. But if you know he's lying, why let it get you all hyped up? Marlon just wants to get under your skin, and you're letting him win. The bigger man shows restraint. Anybody can come down to third level. Not every man can rise to the level of maturity. I thought you were the wiser one, taking those advanced classes and all. But I don't know. Looks like your head is screwed on just as wrong as the dude carrying the knife. Get it together, man."

As I walked to my car holding my eye, I had a bad head-ache. What a day it had been. I didn't know if I was dreaming or not when I saw the most beautiful girl ever leaning against my car. It was Tori. When I realized I wasn't dreaming, I didn't know how to feel about it.

What was she waiting by my ride for? I ain't really have nothing to say to her. I had already acted stupid where she was concerned. It was time for me to wise up, 'cause being around her was not going to help me.

"Excuse me, but I gotta go."

"W-Wait a minute. I need to talk to you. I heard during cheerleading practice that Marlon hurt you. I'm so sorry."

"Yeah. Sure you are."

She tried to look at my face, but I just pulled away. Her concern was a little too late for me. She could tell by my actions that I wasn't feeling her right then.

"You need to go on with your new dude. I gotta go. My dad's waiting on me at the hospital to check out my eye."

"Oh, my gosh! You're going to the hospital!" she said. "Perry, I got your message. I realized too late that you really do care for me."

"I made it clear how I felt on your answering machine. You didn't need to get with another dude to make me jealous. It didn't make our situation any better when you weren't denying what was said this morning, either."

I opened up my car door and got in. I tried to shut it, but she somehow got in the way, preventing me from shutting it.

"What do you mean?" she asked, touching the injured side of my face. "You know me. I couldn't respond because I was shocked to see you fighting for me. I'm not saving myself because I wanna hurt you. And you think I would rather give it up to some guy I just went out with, huh? I'm saving myself because God wants me to. You should've known he was lying, Perry. I didn't say anything to defend myself. You didn't defend me, either. You just stood there."

"I did say something. I forgot what I said, but I did look at you to verify that he was lying. That was your cue right there.

You made me think all day that he took your innocence. That really hurt, Tori."

All of a sudden, I felt her soft lips against mine. She had the most perfect kiss: sweet, gentle and passionate. I made the kiss last for a while. And at that moment I knew everything that I'd been thinking about her being with somebody else wasn't true. All her passion was still for me.

"You my girl or what?" I asked as I pulled my lips from hers.

"Always," she said before we kissed again.

A few days later, it was the first game of the season. I still had a bandage on my eye. But thankfully everything was going to heal. The scouts were in the stands, watching, from what my dad had told me. And for the first half, I did not put on a show for them. I couldn't seem to get my mojo flowing. I was dropping balls, and I even ran a wrong route. My head just wasn't in the game.

At halftime, Coach broke it down to me that this was my time to shine. He was putting the balls in my hand as we trailed at home 17-0. Second half I scored three touchdowns. I jumped over two defenders and did a backflip into the end zone. The only thing I could do was thank God when the clock ran out and we won 21-17.

I hadn't done enough of that. I hadn't spent a lot of time with Him. But when things were shaky, I knew He drove out the strength that I held deep inside. And for that, I was grateful.

I acknowledged Him again as I silently prayed. *I don't even know if I'm doing this right. But thanks for giving me the life You've given me, Lord.*

Damarius came running on top of me. "Man, we're praying in the middle of the field with the other team. Come on, let's go! Coach Robinson is starting here a FCA thing."

"FCA?"

"Fellowship of Christian Athletes, I think. Come on, man. You suppose to pray with everybody else."

Praying twice didn't seem like a bad thing. It actually seemed pretty good. No one had got seriously hurt. Plus, sportsmanship was all over the place. Another prayer of thanks seemed in order.

Coach Robinson led the prayer.

"Most high God, we come to You this evening to give thanks. We're thankful for this contest. We thank You for these young men that are assembled here today. Happy that You kept them healthy. Very thankful that You allowed us to be fortunate enough to participate in a game like football. With all these things, we appreciate the fact that You sent your Son, Jesus, to die on a cross for all our sins. I don't know where these young men stand with You. But I pray right now, Lord, above football, the girls or anything else in this world that holds their interest, they would have a love for You. Help them all find You if they don't know You. Help strengthen the ones that have a relationship with You that aren't where You want it to be. Help them know and appreciate that You make them wake up in the morning. You're the one with the power. May they live to please You, and strive to make You proud. In Jesus's name."

After that prayer, stuff was a blur. I did a lot of interviews, talked to a few scouts, my parents praised me, and I even got another kiss from Tori. But above all of that, I had a private moment that meant a lot to me. I remembered the two prayers after the game, the personal one and the one prayed for me by Coach Robinson. And I knew there was something bigger that I needed to start thinking about.

It wasn't all about me and where my senior year was leading or what school I was going to choose. It was about God. Without putting Him on my agenda I was messing things up, being out of order. Just letting personal things bring my whole life down a negative hill. But with God being my top priority, things were good. And it felt good being in control.

Fighting Every Minute

"Gosh, what did you do? Take five showers?" Tori grumbled as I came out of the locker room after the first game.

I was so looking forward to being with her. Sharing a quiet night, just the two of us. We had a couple of hours before curfew to enjoy each other. I wanted to ensure that Tori and I were back on the same page. But then I come out to all this drama. What the heck was that about? She had sorta ruined it. I guess my face showed it as I looked at her like she was crazy.

"Tori, come on, I don't need this right now. You know we won a game. I was in there talking to my boys and reporters and stuff."

Thinking about the fact that my girl couldn't understand me, or give me the benefit of the doubt sometimes, made me take a real deep breath. I started walking around her and she had to catch up with me.

"I'm sorry! I'm sorry! I'm sorry," she said, stopping me dead in my tracks, preventing me from walking any further. "Please, let's start again. I want to celebrate with you. You had an awesome game."

Grabbing her by her waist and pulling her toward me, I lightly kissed her on the cheek. My lips made it down to her ear and I said, "You know I wanna be with you. Tonight we're gonna really celebrate."

She took my hand and led me to my car. "Not in front of the world," she said as I tried touching the back of her cheerleading skirt. She moved my hand back up her spine some.

"So, what? You just tryin' to play with me tonight?"

Ignoring my question, she said, "Briana's having a party at her house. Let's just go over there."

"Wait, wait, wait . . . a party? I don't wanna be with no crowd. You just said we couldn't do nothing in front of people."

"It's only a small party, baby. Cole's gonna be there, Ciara and Damarius. Not a house party-party. Just a few of us."

"Baby, that's not what I was planning. I wanted to be alone with you. Completely alone. You agree?" I bent down to try and kiss her, but she pulled away.

"No, Perry. I don't wanna be with you alone. It's only gonna lead to trouble for us."

"Trouble? You being with me alone is going to lead to trouble? I don't even understand that. What are you saying?"

Before we could even get into it further, Cole tried to jump on my back.

"Boy, is you crazy? You too big for all of that! We got another game next week. I don't need any injuries."

"Marlon couldn't do it, so I might as well get the job done," he teased. "Better be glad I don't have a knife, boy!"

"Oh, I see, you a comedian now!"

"Come on, man. We headed over to my girl's house. She havin' a big jam."

"I thought it was just going to be a few people," I said, looking at Tori.

Cole gave me a look like, *Come on. Be real.* "We just had our first game, man," he voiced. "Now I believe it's time to par-tayyy! Tori, Briana is over there waiting on you. She said y'all need to go over to her house and get things ready. I'm 'bout to run to the store with Perry."

"Cole, I was not headed to your girl's house, man," I said, as Cole seemed to not take no for an answer.

Tori and I looked at each other. We weren't connecting, and that was frustrating. It was actually good to see her walk away. Cole and I stopped off at the Piggly Wiggly and bought sodas. He tried to pick up some beer, saying he had a fake ID to buy it with.

I told him, "Naw, I ain't buying that for you."

"You such a wuss, man," he said in a stern tone.

"Whatever, man. I ain't about to lose my potential scholarship for no misdemeanor," I responded, standing my ground. "And I'm not letting you go down like that, either."

"Yeah, right. That ain't the only reason. You ain't never even tasted the stuff."

"And I'm not about to taste it now, either. Let's go."

In the cash register line, there were two girls right behind us. I had never seen them before, but Cole said that they went to our school. Cute lil' brown sugars. One had cornrows with a lil' meat on her bones, and her friend had creamy, beige skin and was stacked. Cole invited them to our party.

I said, "Man, are you crazy? Our girls gon' be there!"

Cole turned around and said, "Y'all know how to behave when we with our girlfriends, right? You ain't gon' embarrass us brothas. Come on and make the party more fun and join us. You honeys liked the game tonight, right?" They both nodded. "Then, you gotta come help us celebrate."

We couldn't get out the store without him inviting six more people to Briana's place. All I wanted was time alone with my girl, and now it was like I was gonna be at the house party of the year or something.

"I ain't buying no more food for all these people you inviting," I said to him.

"Oh, yeah. I got that, I got that." Cole turned around and announced to the store, "It's BYOF time!"

"What, boy?" someone shouted.

"Bring Your Own Food. Come on, Cuz. Act like ya know."

When we got to Briana's house, there were cars everywhere. I knew I shouldn't have let none of them talk me into coming. I was heated.

"See, I can tell you ain't happy that we 'bout to throw down in here. We just won our first game and you ready to spoil everything. Come on, bruh. Relax!" Cole said.

"It's Tori, man. I just didn't want my night to go down like this, all right?"

"I'm trying to tell you don't sweat that she ain't putting out yet. You can take care of that and still be with her. Then you wouldn't be so uptight when she tell yo butt 'No!'"

I put up my hand, got out the car, locked the door and carried the groceries inside.

"All right. You don't have to do it my way. One of these days you gon' get tired of making yourself happy," he said, wiggling his hand.

I pushed him. "Boy, you so stupid."

"I'm just real, Perry. Satisfied and real!" he said to me before yelling through Briana's house. "We here, everybody. Let's get the party started!"

Cole went on his way, not getting me at all. I mean, I wanted sex, but I only wanted it with one person. To me it wasn't about a 'Wham, bam, thank you for satisfying me" kinda thing. I wanted to feel something deep. It didn't have to be love, but it had to be something meaningful.

And Cole should've known the solution for him wasn't adding up for me. He could tease me. I was still pure, and I was cool with that. Wasn't sayin' I was proud of it, but I figured once I found Tori, said the necessary things to get her excited, we could blow this joint and celebrate my way. But before I could get to her, Amandi came and took the groceries from my arms and put them in a chair. She was jerking her body from side to side and pushed me down on the sofa.

"Word's out that you want some. I spotted an empty bedroom. Let me make you feel good."

She just didn't know her offering it up like that was a turnoff. I didn't know what I was thinking the first time I saw her. She was fine back then, but now she seemed trashy. Didn't the girl have more respect for herself than to just give it away like that? But it didn't matter what I was thinking. I had gotten caught by my girl in a very compromising situation. And Tori read all kinds of stuff into it.

Next thing I knew Tori threw a pillow at Amandi's back . . . It was on then!

"What you doing all up on my man? What's up?" Tori shouted at Amandi.

"Please! Everybody know y'all are through. Plus, you're with Marlon, the Knife Boy. Perry is free, and I'm 'bout to change all that," she said before getting back on my lap.

I had to push her back, though. She didn't speak for me. Seeing two ladies go at it because of me wasn't making me feel good.

"Amandi, Tori is my girl," I spoke up.

Tori pointed for me to follow her outside. We walked away. There were so many people in that house. My head was hurting from how hot and sweaty it was getting.

When I found my way outside, I said to Tori, "All right, can we blow this place now?"

"I told Briana I'd help her since her folks know I'm spending the night over here. Why can't you stay beside me? Why you have to be all out so those girls can think you're by yourself?" she asked.

"We don't have to put on a show for nobody. We can leave,

and I'll bring you back when the party's done. I thought we wanted the same thing."

"It's supposed to be about us being together, Perry. And we're together right now."

"Naw, that's not what I reassigned for. I mean, I knew we were gon' take things slow, and I'm okay with that. But even with that, I just want some time alone with you."

"It's just gonna lead us to trouble," she sighed.

Cole came grabbing me for help. My girl got away. I was upset, feeling like Tori and I were only together for appearances. By the disgusted look on my face as I came back inside, all the ladies in the house knew that me and Tori's thing wasn't that solid. I wasn't down with forcing myself on anybody. Tori made me feel like she wasn't ready to get anything going.

All night I watched her. She smiled at me, and that was nice. We danced, and that was cool. She kept putting up a fight when I wanted us to spend time alone. That wasn't gon' cut it. I needed to figure this "getting back together thing" out. Maybe I had made a mistake.

My dad was up when I walked through the door. "Boy, I told you to be in this house at 1:30. It's 1:45! And you strolling up in here like you're grown or something."

"Dad, I'm just fifteen minutes late. It's not that big a deal. I had to help get Cole out of trouble."

"What you mean, get him out of trouble? Y'all been drinking or something?"

"Naw, Dad. You know I'm not into that."

"Boy, I don't know what you're into. Saw you at the game, told you what time to be home, and you broke that. Your mother and I have been up worrying about where you were. You don't call, and you don't even answer your cell phone.

And then you walk up in here like it's no big deal. Guess you figure you don't owe us an explanantion. I'm not having it! You will respect my authority as long as you live in my house."

"Fine, Dad, I'm in trouble. Just give me my punishment tomorrow," I said as I walked past him, ready to lay my head on the bed.

"Boy, if you don't bring your behind back here right now . . ."

I turned around and walked back toward my father. He was mad, but I was furious with the fact that he was blowing these few minutes out of proportion. And for what? I wasn't messing up in no kinda way. He had a good son compared to most.

When my friends want to get drunk, some of my boys sneak in a lil' somethin' somethin', and I haven't gotten with that. I even have some teammates that slip and slide with different girls, but I don't do none of that, and my dad still trippin'. He didn't even realize what he's got: a great son. Let Cole or Damarius switch places with me for a day. Then he'd be grateful for what he's got. But in a few more months, I'll be gone and I'll never have to worry about his stupid rules ever again.

"You know what, boy? Just go to bed," he said as I walked back over. "We'll talk about this tomorrow and I'm taking your keys."

We never said good night to each other. We never apologized. We just sauntered to our own rooms and stood our own ground. I wasn't a lil' boy anymore. My dad's voice couldn't shake me anymore.

My parents' room wasn't right down the hall, it was downstairs. So I couldn't believe it when I was awakened to the two of them arguing early Saturday morning. Dragging myself downstairs, I had to get down there to see what was going on. I knew my folks' relationship hadn't been all good lately, but arguing in the house was something I had never heard them do. I figured if I let them see me, then they would cease screaming.

However, I was frozen in my tracks when I heard my mother say, "You act like I don't know what's best for our son."

"I'm not saying you don't know what's best for him, you just keep babying the boy!" my dad said loudly.

Aww, snap! They were arguing about me, I realized. Truly, I didn't want to be the cause of tension between them.

"Junior needs to be looking at a school that's gon' challenge his mind, like Duke or Georgia Tech. Those were my top choices," my mom said.

My dad said, "If that boy is going to school for football, then he's going to have to go somewhere where he doesn't have to pray to get out. Yeah, he's smart but if he takes that knowledge to a school where academics isn't so overbearing, then he's gonna come out great. It's like you trying to make the boy fail."

"Well, honey, he's not going to school to major in football. What if he gets hurt? I mean, let's be realistic here. Most of those boys who are recruited in high school do not go on to maintain professional careers in their sport. I want our son to have something else to fall back on. Actually, not something to fall back on, but something that is his top priority. And *he* needs to make this decision. *You* chose where you wanted to go to school."

"That boy don't know what he's doing. He definitely needs his father in this process. And it's clear to me that his mama don't need to have nothing to do with it," my father boasted. "He doesn't need to go to a school where they don't even have business as a major. You know I want him to take over the dealership one day."

That was news to me. Payton always wanted that job. And my dad made her feel like it was hers. Now he was saying he wanted me to take up the family buisness. Wonder when he was going to ask me?

He continued, "You're not even acknowledging that he's a great football player. The top player in the state right now, Patricia. He needs to ride the football thing until the ride ends. You're trying to make him get off of it before it stops. Believe in your son."

My mom put her hand up in front of my dad. I guess she wanted him to hush up. He grabbed her arm harshly. It was something about the way he grabbed it that made me snap. I dashed inside the kitchen area and pushed my father back with hard force. I'd never used that on him before. It was like defending a free safety or something.

"Boy, have you lost your mind?" my dad yelled as he turned and grabbed me by the collar. "I wasn't gon' hurt your mama. We're just in here talking."

His lil' grip wasn't bothering me at all. I just didn't want my dad to think that I was scared of him. I know what I saw, and I know what I heard. And my mom's reaction showed she was very uncomfortable.

"Let him go, Junior! You two stop that," my mother ordered.

I didn't know why my mama was telling me to stop. I wasn't doing anything. I was just standing there boldly while my dad had my shirt shriveled all up in his hand. I hated the fact that I was named after my father in times like these.

Only around my parents did I not get to be who I normally was, and that was Perry. I had to answer to Junior, and he got to hold the name. I didn't know why my father and I were drifting apart so, but when I looked at him I could only pray, *"Lord, help us."*

"Son, let me tell you. The next time you come at me like a man, I'm gon' take off my belt and show you that you're still a boy. You understand me?"

I said nothing. I wasn't trying to disrespect him, but at this time I felt he didn't deserve my respect. So I said nothing. I mean, what was he gon' do? Really take off his belt and make me say something? I just looked at him. He came over toward me, and my mom got in his way.

"Let him go," my mother said. "Son, go on to your room now. Go, go!"

I had no problem following that order. I still couldn't believe what had just occurred. Breathing deeply, I retreated to my room and wished things were different.

For the next two days my father and I avoided each other. Monday morning when I was ready to head to school in my car, I noticed I didn't have my keys. My dad had talked about taking the car, but I didn't pay it no mind since I'd driven it yesterday. Why was he trippin'?

"Mom, where are my keys?"

All of a sudden, my dad walked into the room jingling the keys. Guess he called himself trying to teach me a lesson.

"Dad, I need my keys or I'm gonna be late for school!" I said without thinking.

"Guess you better call one of your boys to come get you or tell your mom to take you. You won't be driving this car for a week."

"All my friends are probably off to school, Dad. Why didn't you tell me last night that you were taking my car?"

"I told you when you came in late Friday night that I was taking your car."

"Why you doing this? I don't need my mom taking me to school; I'm not in kindergarten. Come on, Dad. I just won't be late for curfew anymore."

"That's not all it's about, Junior. You've been acting mighty grown around here lately. You might be good on the football field, but you stepped incorrectly to me the other day. I haven't heard any apology from you yet."

"I thought you was messing with my moms. You're the one who taught me to defend her and my sister, no matter who it was."

"And I see you trying to be a smart aleck again. You better find you a way to school, and, Patricia, don't you dare take him. He thinks it's beneath him to get a ride from a parent, let him figure it out on his own. Everything he's got and everything on his back, our money bought for him. And, what? He gon' challenge me? I'm tired of fussing with the boy."

"Honey, I hear you but school is important, so I'm taking him to school."

"No, I *said* don't take him."

"No! I'm taking him to school. Junior, let's go."

I was smiling on the inside. By the look on my father's face, he wasn't pleased, though. He started talking some more mess, and I blocked it all out because my mom was taking me to school. In my mind, I had won.

But as we got in the car and drove in silence I realized maybe I hadn't won at all. Maybe I had just driven a bigger wedge between my parents. I felt worse than if I'd been hit by a Mack truck.

I, too, was tired of arguing with my father, but that was just our life now. He thought he ruled everything, but he didn't rule me. If I had to be uncomfortable or make my mom uncomfortable, then so be it. Taking my car and my keys for a week, my dad was crazy. But even though I didn't agree with him, he still was the one calling all the shots. Shoot! I wasn't walking, but I wasn't driving, either. I was riding in the car with my moms to school. A senior. Captain of the football team. A guy being recruited by several schools. A guy most girls in my school want to get with, and I had to get a ride with my moms. Wasn't that a trip!

"Let's ride over to Paine College," Damarius said as Cole drove around Augusta after football practice.

"Yo, I'm tired. Take me home," I said to the two of them.

"Boy, when you ain't drivin', you don't get to decide where to go, last time I checked," Damarius said from the passenger side.

I retorted, "Last time I checked, you weren't drivin', either."

"Aww, come on, man. You gotta roll with us over to Paine so we can hit up those freshmen girls D and I met last night," Cole said, revealing the real plan.

"Heck, naw! I ain't going to see no girls on campus—what? I just got my flow back together with Tori, and I ain't tryin' to add no drama to the situation. Just take me home."

"You a punk, man," Damarius said as he turned around to me.

From the backseat, I sat up and squeezed his neck. "What the heck you say?"

"Come on, y'all," Cole said as he started swerving the car. "Let him go, Perry, man! Let him go."

"No!"

Cole took the car onto the side of the road. We barely missed hitting two cars, thanks to his driving. He slammed on his brakes, stopped the car and pulled my hands from his pal's trembling body.

Damarius started coughing. "I don't know what's gotten into you, man," he turned around and said to me.

"I'm sick and tired of people telling me what I need to do with my life. I wanna go home. I'm not tryin' to chase no skirt. You know I'm on punishment. Besides, I'm surprised none of y'all negroes ain't got one of these girls pregnant or

caught a disease, as much as y'all try to get with every girl
y'all see. I got other stuff on my mind than trying to add
more girl problems to the list."

Damarius rubbed his neck. "Take him home, then, Cole, if
it's like that."

I made sure they both knew I wasn't with their games.
"It's like that."

Being at home doing my homework was hard. I was used
to having my own car: go where I wanted to go and do what
I wanted to do. But now I had to get a ride with my friends. I
could've called Tori, but . . . I don't know. Guess I was just
tired of arguing. I could've begged my dad for my keys back
and apologized, told him I'd learned my lesson. Naw, that
wasn't too appealing, either.

Just when I thought my night was going to be boring,
there was a knock on the door. It was Damarius and Cole. I
really did regret the car brawl. I deeply hoped we could work
it out.

"I figured since we got all these recruiting meets coming
up, there was no need to keep this stress between us," Cole
said as I opened the door.

"No, I'm glad y'all here. D, I shouldn't have grabbed your
neck like that, man."

Damarius responded, "No, I shouldn't have called you a
punk. I pushed you too far."

It was cool that the two of us could relate, but I had to
drop a bomb on them. I told them they couldn't keep going
with me to recruiting visits. That was another thing my father
had made clear over the last couple of days. The meetings
were limited to me and my family only. Since Cole had already committed to South Carolina, I didn't think that he
would be too broken up about it, which turned out to be the
case. But Damarius went off on me.

"See, man, you making everything personal. We came over here to apologize, you grabbed my neck, and now you wanna tell me I can't come along for the ride to try and get schools interested in me! I know once I show the coaches what I got, the stuff on film, they will wanna sign me on the spot. And now you taking that chance away from me. That ain't cool, Perry. That ain't cool."

"What you talking 'bout? This don't have anything to do with me," I told him.

I was sick and tired of having to carry the two of them. Yeah, they were my boys and all, but dang! Cole had found his way. Why couldn't Damarius let it go and find his? If he had shown enough on film himself and had better grades, he'd have opportunities.

I said, "Call up the coaches, then. Give them your case personally."

"Like anybody is going to answer my phone calls."

"I didn't make the rules. Me and my dad are having some issues right now. I'm not rocking the boat more, D," I said.

"All you need to do is tell your dad it doesn't matter what the school says. If you come with twenty people, and they want you bad enough, they will accommodate and give you twenty game tickets. The schools will let your guests eat the food, tour the campus, anything. The red carpet is gon' be laid out for you and anyone you want to bring."

"My father didn't want me to push schools like that. He and I, as I just said, are having issues and I don't want to force this. Cole is already straight. You may not get to go to a Division 1 school. It ain't like the world's going to end."

Damarius got up close to me with watery eyes. "Easy for you to say. You got a ton of 'em you can choose from, but now my choices are limited 'cause you won't stand up for your boy. Come on, Cole, man, I don't even know why we came over here."

"Hey, you just showing me your true colors. Why would I want to stand up for somebody that gets mad when I can't give them what they want?"

"It's just my future, Perry," Damarius said with passion.

"So, then show it on the football field. We got eight or nine more games! I can't get you into a college; you gotta do it for yourself."

"You could try."

"I took you to South Carolina, man. You were loud, rude, chasing skirts—you were a little embarrassing."

"Oh, so now I'm embarrassing? Cole, let's go, man. Let's go!" Damarius shouted at our friend.

"So, you think I'm wrong, too, Cole?" I asked as he went to the door.

"Hey, I'm out of this. I just know you two need to see each other's side. I can understand and appreciate both of them."

Damarius went on down the driveway, talking loud, obnoxious stuff. I didn't hear half of what he was saying. In his own weird way, he was telling me off. But you know where he was saying it—not in my face.

I had no problems walking in the hallways alone. This year Tori's classes were way on the other side of the school, so we agreed to just see each other at lunch and after practice. Most mornings she found me, and I gave her a peck. However, for the most part I walked alone. Today, though, my friend Justin came up next to me.

"Yo, man, why you been avoiding me?" Justin questioned.

"What you talkin' about?" I asked.

Justin explained. "We get out of one class together and then when we head to the next together, you leave so fast like you embarrassed to be seen with me or somethin'. I thought we cleared all that mess up about you was gon' let me hang out with you a little more so I can feel the hint of popularity. You reneging on that promise?"

Why does everybody think the world revolves around them? No matter what I do, it's never enough for my friends. Folks always wantin' stuff from me. Schools wantin' me to sign, girls wantin' my time, and now this knucklehead thinks I can make him popular.

"It was not a fluke at the party, man. You were a hit to be with because of how you were acting. Just be you. You're smart and you're great. Quit thinking you need to hang with me for everything. I got my own issues. And trust me, man; my space isn't all that good right about now."

"Yeah, I heard you didn't wanna help yo boy get into college."

"What? That's the word that's going around? How you gon' believe that crap, anyway? Damarius is flunking out of school and getting beat on many long passes. If he wants to go to college he better pass the SAT and worry 'bout his own game."

Justin said, "Hey, I'm simply saying that just 'cause you got it going on, doesn't mean you can't worry about your friends."

Justin walked off from me. That was a good thing, too, 'cause if he would've stayed in my face it would've been on! I was sick of Tori. I was sick of Damarius. I was sick of my dad. Now I was sick of Justin. Shoot, I was sick and tired of being sick and tired.

Being Perry Skky Jr. was a lot. Too many expectations. I didn't mind doing favors sometimes, but I couldn't please everybody all the time. However, I was going to have to get a grip on it; I'd have to figure out a way to be back in control. I was tired of fighting every minute.

~ 5 ~

Yielding to Others

I was now in a good routine. School had been in for a while. I had adjusted to my tougher classes, understood what the coaches expected, and our team was clicking. We were winning games. We hadn't lost one yet. I didn't mind being at practice and giving 100 percent. The outcome was paying off in a big way. Colleges were still calling. And I was still the man.

I was feeling real lonely, though. Tori and I were still an item but we hadn't really figured out how we were gon' work this thing. My dad and I were cordial toward each other. He'd given me my car back, but we weren't the best of friends or anything. And my boys—though Cole and I were cool, I hadn't seen much of him or Damarius. So, when Damarius and I ran a drill together for Coach Robinson, I eased off and let my old buddy get all the glory.

A teammate shouted, "Ooh! Sweet interception, Damarius. Do it, boy!"

Yeah. Letting him catch the ball instead of me seemed to inflate his spirit. He'd been moping around practice for the past couple of weeks and he had a horrible game last Friday. Thankfully, he didn't lose it for us, but he did get benched, and I wanted him to get his starting job back. All he needed was his confidence. The boy talked so much smack and didn't deliver. He needed to know he could bring it if given the opportunity. If he tried to look for the opportunity, he could make some big plays.

"Dang, boy, you beat me on that one," I said when we got to the sidelines. Coach Robinson didn't let me say much more after he chewed me out for falling asleep on the play. I just sorta smirked and said, "Yes, Coach. I gotcha."

Coach Robinson looked at me eye to eye. I didn't wanna give away what I was doing. I didn't want all that Damarius had felt to be taken away from him because it was called out that I missed the play on purpose.

So I said, "Coach, I'ma do better next time. He just beat me, that's all."

"Yeah, okay. You better do better next time. Damarius, good job, son. That's the kinda action I need to see Friday night."

When practice was over, Damarius came over to me and said, "Dang, man, I didn't mean to do you like that today!"

"Naw, cuz you beat me fair and square," I said as we slapped hands.

"Sorry we haven't been connecting lately. Perry, I miss hanging out, man," he said to me. "I've just been having some issues lately that I've been meaning to run by you. Can we talk? We still boys, right?"

"Always," I told him as we slapped hands again and hugged.

"Oh, look at the two of y'all! Friends again, huh?" Cole asked as he came in between us and put us both in a headlock.

"That hurts!" I said.

Damarius yelled, "Come on, Cole, man!"

"Well, I'm going let the two of y'all handle it. Briana and I are about to head and get some ice cream or somethin'," Cole joked in a mischievous way.

"Be smart, partner, and I'll take the knucklehead home," I said. Damarius usually rode home with Cole.

When we got in the car, it was time for me or Damarius to initiate conversation. It had been such a while since the two of us had been together that our flavor didn't feel like usual. I knew I needed to break down and be the bigger man and apologize for some things I'd said to him. He didn't deserve me reducing him to nothing the last time we were in my house. Though that wasn't my intention, I knew it could have been perceived that way.

So I said, "Hey, man. About the whole recruiting thing, I'm sorry."

"You were right, Perry. You said some things I needed to hear. Can't depend on you to get into college. That catch today proved I gotta show up. I gotta play on Friday nights. I've gotta get the scouts to look at me, you know. I know you're a good friend, Perry, and I know you'd do anything for me, but you're right about me doing stuff for myself. But there are some things I need your help with."

"What, man? What's going on?" I could tell he had a heavy heart.

Whispering he said, "I couldn't mention this in front of Cole because he'd probably laugh or rag on me to the whole team. But, it's pretty serious. Lately, I've been having a burning sensation every time I use the bathroom."

I had no idea Damarius was trying to talk to me about some personal situation like that. He was creeping me out. However, I stayed calm, kept the car on the road and listened. Now I knew why even though it was just the two of us in the car, he was speaking softly. This couldn't get out.

He continued, "Ciara went to the doctor, and she got gonorrhea. They said it has to be something I gave her. I know she's only been with me. I've only been with two others: that girl in college and some other girl that ain't even in school. I don't know which one of them gave it to me, but I think I need to go get checked out. The joint is hurting. I don't know where to go, though. You know I don't have a ride or cash to take care of it."

"Don't you still got that Medicaid card your dad gave you?" I asked, remembering he had showed it to me last year.

"Yeah."

"Well, let's go see the team doctor. I know where his real practice is."

Holding his head down, my buddy said, "You don't think he'll . . . laugh at me or somethin'?"

"Man, please. He looks at that stuff for a living. Let's ride over to see if he can see you real quick."

Dr. Hanceby was a real cool white dude. He loved football, too. Told us if we had any physical problems that we could see him anytime.

"I don't know, Perry, man. I'm a lil' nervous," Damarius said as we pulled into the parking lot of the doctor's office.

Thankfully, Dr. Hanceby hadn't left for the day; he saw us both. I was in one room and Damarius was in the other. He came in to my room.

"Do you need me to check you down there, too?" he asked.

"Oh, no! I'm straight there, sir. Just my eye. Want to make sure my cut is healed."

"Yeah, right. Your partner over there tells me that you have been having a bit of fun, too."

"No, that couldn't be what he's been telling you because I've been a good boy."

"Come on now, Perry. I know all the girls are throwing themselves at you. Some of these STDs are hard to detect; they don't have symptoms, and you need to be tested."

"Doc, man, I'm serious! I'm straight."

"Okay," he said reluctantly as he looked at my eye. "I see you still have a nice gash there."

"Yes, and it's still tender to touch."

He doctored on it a bit, and then gave me some new ointment. He still looked at me like I needed to confess. I didn't feel comfortable talking about my sexual life with him. But he was a doctor. I knew folks were guilty by association. Since Damarius was brought in under those circumstances, the doc insisted I was lying. But when he kept pushing even after I told him I wasn't with the multiple partner thing yet, or any partners at all, for that matter, he didn't come up off me until I blurted out that I was a virgin.

"All right, I think that's great. Abstinence is definitely the best answer."

Oddly I felt less significant in his eyes admitting that. "You think I'm a punk, huh?"

"With the skills you got on the field, man, there's no way I could think that. I actually admire you. You could be playing with young ladies' minds, but you're not doing that."

"I am trying to be sexually active, but my girl's not ready."

"You do know what to do when she is, right? Even though it may be the first time for both you guys, you have got . . ."

Cutting him off before he gave me the condom talk, I said, "I'm straight, Doc."

"Well, come to me with any questions. About your boy having an STD, he said I could talk to you about it," Dr. Hanceby said. Man, I hated Damarius had dragged me in it. "He's going to be on medication for a while, and he's gotta keep stuff to himself for a bit as well. Sex is nothing to play with; you don't know who's been with whom. So to avoid all that, help him do what you're doing. Trust me, you have plenty of time to be grown up . . . later on. Right now enjoy what you got going on: football and school. I wish all teens could get by without sex."

"Again, Doc, I'm not all proud of that or anything. I'm not trying to tell the world that I'm a virgin."

"You should be proud, though. That status is more impressive than any catch you could ever make. Knowing that you're not pushing your girl to do something she doesn't want to do or not leaving for not doing it makes me respect you even more."

I heard all that he was saying. I didn't deserve all his respect. I certainly wanted to push Tori to give me what I thought I needed. Maybe he was telling me that I was cool the way I was. As I walked out empty-handed and Damarius came out with his hands full of pills that he was going to have take for a lil' bit, I knew my way was better.

"Don't say I told you so," he said to me.

"Look, I'm just glad gonorrhea's all you got and you caught it early. How about that? My lips are sealed."

"Thanks, man," Damarius said, as he nodded, agreeing his fate could have been much worse.

We rode home in silence as we pumped up the music, bopped our heads and cruised down the street. I was glad he got his medicine, and I was glad that I wasn't a playboy. Being Damarius's friend again taught me up close and personal that not getting some action was definitely a good thing.

Friday night lights were here and up again. The coach called me to his office after the team had our dinner.

"Before we get on the road and travel to Greene County for this game, I want to tell you, son, that I've been watching you during practice. You make the players feel like they're better than they really are. You haven't been catching the catches I know you can, so others around here can look good. I hope that doesn't show in your performance tonight."

"Oh, no, sir. I haven't been doing that."

"Cut the bull. You've done it and a ton of times. But it's actually commendable; it's giving them something they need: hope. You've raised your level of playing. And even with Marlon back, you two have not been so adversarial, and I know that's because of your leadership. I want you to give the pregame speech to the team. Just tell them that there's no "I" in the word. Can you do that?"

"Yes, sir."

Thirty minutes later, the team was all huddled close to hear what I was going to say to motivate them. We'd been operating pretty well as a team. Neither Coach nor I wanted that to change going into hostile territory.

Cautiously I said, "I am the captain of this team. And I know over the last couple of weeks it's been said in the papers that I've won the game for us after a catch here or a run there. However, I don't believe that hype. We won the last three games because this team has been phenomenal. Defense has had offense's back when we couldn't score. Our kicker hasn't missed one all season long, special teams have always put us in great field positions, and our quarterback is the bomb. Now we've got another weapon to throw. You know Marlon ain't my favorite person, but he's a heck of a football player. And if we all come together and put our pride, our differences, our own special talents aside, and play for the good of the team, then no one will be able to stop us. Not even these snotty rich boys we 'bout to play tonight. So when you're riding there on the bus, think about doing your best for the team. If we all play our best, it's a victory fo' sho."

"We can beat 'em!" Damarius shouted.

* * *

Three hours later we were playing in front of a packed stadium for the home team. As soon as we stepped on that field we showed them who was for real. We showed them we were a team on a mission. We played as a unit and threw down.

Damarius had an interception. Our quarterback ran one in himself for a touchdown. Special teams blocked a field goal for the other team that made us shut them out. Defense forced a safety. When we were together, we were unstoppable. Together, we scored 51 points. I had the least catches and yards I've ever had in a ball game, but we won by the most points. Teamwork was something impressive to see in action.

When the coach came up to me and gave me the game ball, I didn't understand. "These guys played like a team tonight, Perry Skky Jr. Because you as a leader showed them that they all were worthy, I give the team ball to you."

"And I give this ball back to the team," I said as I looked around at them holding the ball in the air.

We all screamed in the locker room like little cheerleaders, but it was all a good thing. It was a hard-fought victory we deserved to be proud of. We took everything and gave up nothing. Everybody stepped up and the scoreboard showed it: 51-0. I'll never forget it.

We had brought four buses up. The football team, cheerleaders and the band had ridden separately. With that dynamic score, the guys had talked our coach into letting the team integrate with friends for the ride back. When I came out the locker room, Tori was patiently waiting on me.

She rushed up to me. "What a great game!"

"Hey, girl. Feel like I ain't seen you in forever," I said as I kissed her on her cheek and spun her around.

It was refreshing to see her cute lil' face. I remembered once during the game we were on defense, I glanced over and saw her jamming to the band's music. I was proud. And to actually have her in my arms at that moment made me think maybe she and I would be okay after all.

"Briana and Ciara are holding us a seat on the last bus," she said. I looked at her, puzzled. "No, you're not just sittin' with my girls; D and Cole are back there, too."

I squinted as I realized she didn't get what I was thinking. "Yeah, I'm sure they are back there, Tori. I'm just wondering if you sure that this is a good idea."

"What?"

"Us going to the back of the bus with them. Do you know what they plan on doing back there?"

"Skky, hurry up, guy," my coach yelled out. "Make a decision so we can we go. Now!"

She leaned over, touched my shoulder and bent me down to her mouth. I didn't know what Tori was about to say. But the look in her eye was totally mischievous, like she was ready to be a bad girl for once.

She said, "I'm ready to be with you. I thought about it. Over the last couple of weeks, we've been sort of distant with each other. I know why. And I love you enough to go further to please you. Let's go."

She took my hand and pulled me to the last bus.

I pulled her back toward me and said, "Umm, come on. We gotta get on the first bus 'cause I gotta talk to you about a couple of things on the ride home."

"The first bus? All the administrators ridin' on that one so nothing can happen on there. Uh-uh, Perry. I'm sure. Seriously, come on."

"Nah, babe. Not this way. I can't." I shocked myself with my statement.

Before I could second-guess my own decision, we were sittin' right behind my coach on the first bus. So much stuff was going on in my head about why I didn't take Tori up on her first offer. I could have had my way with her on that last bus.

Maybe it was Damarius's run-in with a sexually transmitted disease. Maybe it was the doctor telling me he was proud of me that I was choosing to stand for something and put my hormones in check. Maybe it was the fact that though I knew what Tori was saying I didn't really believe it.

She had been so strong to stand her ground for not wanting to go that way. Certainly, if she was ready, she would not want her first time being in front of a whole bunch of people. I had to protect her from herself. I had to protect us from giving something that we were not willing to get back. And deep down, I also wanted to please God. He had been blessing me this year with so much. Part of me didn't wanna be ungrateful by going against His wishes.

Tori looked out the window and said, "What's wrong with you? I thought that's what you wanted."

I grabbed her hand and gripped it really tight. "A month ago, that was all I thought about and all I ever wanted. But now, I need more than that. You're right. We did drift apart, and I wanna get that back on track before we go making it all physical. I don't want you to regret it, either. I want our first time to be right." I kissed her on the cheek and she laid her head on my shoulder.

Halfway through the ride, she looked up at me with tears in her eyes. "Thank you." She smiled. "I don't really know if I was ready, but I don't wanna lose you. So, thanks."

I rubbed the top of her head as she laid back on my chest. I never said one word to Coach, but his head was nodding as he turned around and looked at me, letting me know he knew why I sat behind him. As he had told me, I did have a responsibility as a leader. Not just on the team, but in my relationship.

One day I hoped to be married and be head of the house

and lead. But I couldn't just suddenly lead one day in a married relationship. I'd have to practice along the way. And though I didn't have it down, I was proud of how I was taking other people into consideration with how I lived my life.

I had only heard about the very beautiful campus Auburn University had. But while driving through the quaint town and seeing all the places, I was like, *Wow! This lil' place has it going on.* It was just me and my parents. And Auburn was set to play LSU at home. It was going to be a great recruiting day.

We followed the signs to the parking lot. When we got there, we were amazed. We pulled right in front of the football facility. There was a shuttle that would take us down to the stadium. But before that, we toured the four-story building.

The practice fields were amazing. I don't know what I expected college to be like. This was only my second recruiting trip, and I was certainly in awe. Before we headed down to the stadium, the wide receiver coach came and talked to us.

He told me, "While your parents meet with the academic advisor, I just wanted to touch base with you quickly and let you know having you as a Tiger would be great. Though you're one of those Georgia boys, this school produces many pro players. And of course the great Bo Jackson won the Heisman from here." He pointed to the powerful brass trophy that I'd love to obtain one day.

"Pat Sullivan, too, right?" I asked, seeing two.

"Correct. You can be the third. Our receivers shine here. They're second to no one. That's why we're really trying to recruit the best."

"Coach, I'm excited to be here. Honestly, I haven't made any decisions yet, but Auburn is a great school. A solid team for years."

"Well, son, we know you've got a sister at Georgia and we're just trying to be honest here. We don't mind rolling out the red carpet for extra-special recruits like you. Ones that we really want to sign with us."

I stepped out onto the practice field and on the big screen was my highlight film. All of a sudden over the loudspeaker I heard my name called. One of the team members came out and handed me a jersey with "Skky" on the back. It looked nice in that blue and orange. All I knew was, Auburn was all right with me.

After we got shuttled over to the stadium, we were directed to a special entrance for recruits that was massive. It was gated off. You couldn't come through unless staff ushered you in. We were greeted by all these pretty hostesses. One girl came and introduced herself to me as a Tigerette. Both me and my dad did a double take when some of those cute girls walked by. We were just joking, but my mom hit us both in the stomach. Finally, my pops and I had connected on something.

"There's the Saxon Lee boy," my mom said. "His mom—she and I talked in South Carolina. Let me go say hello."

My dad and I connected again. He was feeling me. I was not excited. My mom shouldn't consort with the enemy. There might be only one spot for a great receiver here. Saxon and I were competing for the same thing.

I looked around and I didn't see Saxon anywhere. My mom went off, though, to chat with the lady. When I turned around I did see a lovely sight: his sister, Savoy. Our eyes caught each other at the same time. She smiled, and it was perfect. Straight, bright whites, all glowing at me. Her mother was introducing her to my mom.

I was just about to head over there and join in on their conversation when an older white man touched my father's shoulder. "Excuse me. Mr. Skky?"

My dad turned around and so did I. It was a guy that looked sorta familiar. I knew him from somewhere.

My father recognized him instantly. "Oh, Reverend Shadrach."

The man said, "This is my son, Lance."

I still was clueless. That name sounded familiar, too. Who were these people? I knew this guy was obviously a recruit. And for a white boy, he looked to have nice size. I wondered what position he was. Everybody was competition.

"Reverend Shadrach, this is my son, Perry. Perry, you know Lance. You hung out at his house a couple of years ago. This is Payton's roommate's brother."

"Oh, yeah. I remember. I had forgotten for a quick second. You guys live in Conyers, Georgia."

Lance shook my hand and said, "Yes, good to see you."

I clearly remembered now: Lance was Laurel's middle brother. Our sisters used to be roommates. They'd both made the Georgia cheerleading squad together and they were still good friends. I'd hung out at that house once briefly.

"Hey, man. You look different," I said to Lance as I noticed his hair was a little longer. "Quarterback, right?"

"Yep and you're a receiver. So Auburn's looking at you, huh?"

"I guess."

"You two need to head in there," my father said as he made us notice the coach in the corner motioning for us. "I think they're calling all recruits to go meet with the coaches before the game."

Lance and I hit it off well. He told me his team was undefeated, Salem High School. I told him that maybe we would meet them in the Dome. He smiled. Before I left that room, I looked back for Savoy. Unfortunately, she was gone.

"I think we're supposed to go this way," Lance said to me when he clearly saw that I wasn't paying any attention.

"Oh, thanks, man."

He teased, "These Tigerettes got you."

"Something better than that," I said, referring to Savoy.

"I catch you lookin' at my sister again, it's gon' be on," a voice from behind me said. I knew it was Saxon.

"You know this guy?" Lance asked.

I joked, "Pssh. Not really. He's one that you don't wanna know, either."

"Yeah, right. Step aside, man. Saxon Lee. You're that quarterback from Conyers, right?"

"Yeah, Lance Shadrach." They shook hands as Saxon sized him up.

"Your sister goes to Auburn? Our sisters go to Georgia," Lance said, trying to put the pieces together.

"Naw, I got a twin sister that's here with me, and I caught this sucker looking at her. And actually, Perry, she'll probably like this dude more than you!"

Lance appeared not to understand. Saxon didn't even know that I knew about his sister liking white boys. Nor did he know that I had a special evening with her, thanks to his cousin Tad. I couldn't say that Savoy was into me, but I knew we had a special connection.

The three of us went on to watch the game together. Auburn and LSU went down to the wire. Thankfully, the Tigers from Auburn pulled it out, not the LSU Tigers. They had to go home with a loss. After the game, Savoy came toward Lance, her brother and me.

"Watch this, Perry. She ain't even gon' say nothing to you. She's gonna talk to him first. Think you got skills, boy? Naw, you ain't her type."

Saxon was full of it, but I just laughed. I don't know why boys always liked to gamble or compete. Why did it always have to be a challenge? But it didn't matter. I didn't even have to sweat it. Savoy walked right by her brother and Lance, and gave me a big hug. Her brother's mouth dropped way to the ground. And then she gave me a kiss on the cheek. It was over for him then!

Saxon cut in between us. "Aww, heck, naw! What you doing kissin' him? You don't even know this boy."

Savoy explained, "Tad's girlfriend—"

"Yeah, Payton, the hot chick."

"—this is her brother." She pushed her brother back.

"You lying? This the dude you went out with?"

Lance and I slapped hands. I didn't wanna seem too cocky in front of the lady. So, I excused myself to both fellas and walked away with Savoy hand in hand.

"So, you like Auburn?" she asked me.

Unable to take my eyes off her, I said, "I like what I see at Auburn."

"Now, I know you ain't flirting with me?" She batted her long eye lashes.

I couldn't even answer the question. For some reason I was really attracted to her. For the first time I wondered if that was the reason why I was having mental pressure about going the extra mile with Tori. Maybe it didn't have anything to do with my girl at all. Maybe it had something to do with saving myself for someone else.

"Flirting isn't bad, is it? I gotta say you look great today."

"Thanks," she said flipping her hair in a way that made me even more into her. "Well, I didn't know when I would see you. We gotta do better and stay in touch. How's that girlfriend of yours?"

"As good as I'm sure that boyfriend of yours is. Maybe we need to get rid of both of them, so it's just you and me." I didn't know where that came from.

"Ha, ha, ha, ha, Perry Skky." She thought I was teasing.

Her brother came over and said something to her, and my dad came over and said something to me. We mouthed bye to each other.

"Boy, you need to be over there impressing these coaches, not over here chasing skirts. What's up?" my dad said as he cornered me.

"Dad, I was just saying hi to a friend. They're related to Tad."

My mom chimed in, "Yeah, I found that out."

My dad was mad I was getting sidetracked. I was supposed to be here to check on the school. Not to check out Savoy Lee. And I was straight with that, since her brother acted like he had issues with that, anyway.

I saw two coaches calling for me to come toward them. I wasn't done wanting to chat with Savoy. But, I'd been learning how to suppress my own desires. I guess I was doing okay yielding to others.

~ 6 ~

Seeking True Purpose

"Lord, I can't believe I'm eighteen today," I said on September twenty-eighth, as I rolled over and looked up at the ceiling.

Being one of the first in class to have a birthday has been real cool over the years. I was always a little bigger and got my license before people, but this birthday made me a little apprehensive about being the first one to turn the big 1-8.

I still lived at home with my parents, and had many months before I was out on my own. But I knew I was a man. I often thought about the possibility of going to war now and how scary that sounded. I thought about being able to vote, hoping I'd make the right choices. Yeah, I'd waited to be eighteen for a long time, and now it was finally here.

I continued:

"Lord, I just pray that I can make You proud. I'm a little confused today even though it should be a great day for me. Maybe it's because I'm not where I need to be in my relationship with You. I don't know what I'm asking, 'cause I don't know if I'm ready to completely commit to do right yet. All that church-going stuff and speaking in tongues and everything just really ain't

*my style right now. But I do have a true heart to
please You. And if You can do anything with that, then
I'm all Yours. Amen."*

My birthday was going by real fast. I didn't have major
plans, but I was surprised that Tori couldn't hang out with
me. She said she had something else to do but would make it
up to me next week. Leave it to my boys to always come
through. Though when they started talking about going to
some abandoned warehouse for a party, I just had to protest.

"Aww, man. Just trust us, Perry. Can't you loosen up a lil'
bit?" Damarius asked.

"We know you don't want anything too wild and you ain't
trying to pick up no chicks. Trust us. We got yo back. It's just
a little party. Relax and have a good time," Cole said.

"Fine, whatever." I just rode and trusted they knew where
to take me.

When we got to their "new spot," cars were everywhere.

"Who's having this party, anyway? And are y'all sure we invited? How did y'all hear about this?"

Damarius didn't answer me. He just got on my cell phone
and called somebody. As soon as we opened up the steel door,
people from everywhere shouted, "Happy Birthday, Perry!
Surprise!" I could've gotten both of those jokers. They had
gotten me so good. Then my sister and my parents walked
up.

"You know I couldn't lose our folks," my sister said as she
hugged me and whispered in my ear. "Tad and Dakari brought
over some of their friends, so the party is off the chain!"

It was a bye week for University of Georgia, so I guess my
birthday came at the right time. Tad came and slapped hands
with me. Dakari and a few other Georgia boys hollered at me
next.

"You see we tryin' to cheat," Dakari joked. "We want you

to come and play for us. But we gon' head to da ATL. We just had to come say Happy Birthday Bulldog-style."

"All right, all right," I said to him as I greeted some of their teammates.

"Enough of all the family stuff, move away!" Damarius joked.

My moms wasn't thinking 'bout him, though. She walked up to me and gave me a big kiss on the cheek. "My baby's getting' so big!"

"Mom, come on." Of course I was embarrassed.

My dad said, "Son, I'm proud of you. I give you a hard time, but it's because I expect great things from you. I don't know what Damarius and Cole are thinkin', but we shutting down at twelve so you better get yo groove on in a hurry." He pulled me close. "Heads up, man, a whole bunch of girls came up to me saying that they're your girlfriend. I don't know what you doing, but you better watch yo back."

I only had one girlfriend I claimed. And I scoured around to try and find her. Before Tori came into my sight, Amandi pulled me to the dance floor. I promise, every time I saw her, her clothes were less and less. It was getting colder and colder outside. The crazy girl had on almost nothing!

"I can't believe my mom let you in here," I said to her.

"Probably when yo mama saw me, I had on more than I have on right now. With all these people around, what she gon' do? Be the po po and lock me in jail?"

"I don't know. She see you coming on to her son, she might try."

"I just wanna give you a birthday dance. I'm just wonder-ing, Perry. When you gonna be ready for some real fun? Everybody knows your lil' girlfriend is a Goody Two-Shoes. Aren't you ready for a nasty girl?"

"No comment, no comment!" I said choking as I pulled away from her embrace. "But I'll hook back up wit' you later for real, for real. I need to look around and check out the crowd."

Before I got too far from her, she touched my behind. The girl was really wild! A little too hot for me.

"There you are," said sweet little Tori who came up to me moments later.

For some reason, I was feeling like she was my little cousin, sister, niece or something. Looking at her didn't turn me on one bit. Yeah, she was cute, but it was like teddy bear cute; something that made you snug at night. And though I'd been the one to put on the brakes in the sex area, she had regained her original thought and made her decision to stay a virgin until she got married.

That was good for her, but that wasn't the birthday present that I had in mind. I danced with her, anyway. A few of the honeys in the place were winking at me. None of them made me want to step away from my girl. But when I looked around and saw Damarius dancing with Savoy, my head did a double take.

"What's she doing here?" I blurted out, forgetting whose arms I was in.

"What's who doing here?" Tori asked me.

"Oh, nothing, babe. Nothing. My moms just wanted to make sure that she got everyone."

"You didn't know she was here? I thought she would've given you a hug when you walked in. I was in the back trying to surprise you and she was posted at the door making sure she didn't miss her baby come to his birthday party."

"Yeah, let me go holla at her now. I'll catch back up with you later, babe."

"All right, boo," she said and then gave me a little peck on the lips.

I watched Savoy laugh with Damarius as her long black

hair twirled in the air with her every movement. I was definitely feeling my oats again looking at that sweet sight. I stepped over to my buddy. When he saw me there he broke apart from Savoy and turned to me.

"D, man. I see you were with my friend," I said, smiling at her.

"Yeah, and she can dance, too. You better handle her for the rest of the night. If Ciara sees me with this hottie, she'll lose her mind in here." Then Damarius bent toward my ear. "Do she know you got a girl in here, too?"

"Oh, yeah, Savoy knows. She and I are just friends, partner. But, watch out for a brotha, all right?" I whispered back.

"I got yo back, man."

Damarius pushed me into Savoy. He placed my hand behind her back. I shoved him. We all laughed. When he was gone, the music changed to a really slow groove. She motioned she was okay with dancing with me.

"I wouldn't have expected you to be at this thing," I said to her.

"My cousin told me about it, and I didn't have nothing else to do," Savoy said nonchalantly. "So me and my girls decided to come to an Augusta party and see how y'all do it."

"That's the only reason, huh?" I asked, playin' with her.

She didn't respond. Just held me as our bodies were in rhythm. It was obvious to me that as I'd just had a conversation with three different women in the last twenty minutes, Savoy Lee struck a nerve with me. She made the hairs on the back of my neck stand up. I didn't know what I was going to do with that feeling. And I didn't think Savoy did, either—because when the next song was a slow jam, too, she made an excuse to get away from me. Of course that intrigued me more.

The rest of the party was straight. It didn't end until

around twelve thirty AM. My dad was having such a good time
with his salesmen that helped chaperone that he slipped
when it came to watching the time.

I was handling eighteen well. I was having a good night
without any of three women going off on each other or me.
But inwardly, my heart had made a choice. Now my mind
had to figure out what I was going to do about it. Until that
decision was made, I decided to just keep everything at a status quo. If I was to be with Savoy, it would work itself out.

"Mom, why do you want me to be in the Beautillion?" I
asked, hoping to ease my way out of this event, given by my
mom's sorority, Delta Sigma Theta. As a big muckety-muck
there, everything they had going on she was a part of it, it
seemed like. And that was cool 'cause I didn't mind my moms
not being home all the time to tend to my every need. She actually gained more flexibility. With Dad being at work, she
could run around saving the world.

It was only when she wanted to include me in that high-
society stuff that a sour taste was left in my mouth. It was
cool for Payton to be a debutante 'cause that was right up her
alley at the time. I didn't want to be a Beaux, but it was like
Moms wasn't giving me a choice.

"Junior, let's be fair here. I support your events all year,
making all your football games, going on your recruiting visits, planning other birthday parties. I'm asking my son to do
one thing for me, and that's being in this Beautillion. I want
to introduce you to society. I want my friends to know how
proud I am of my baby! Plus, they teach so many great things
throughout the process. It's like your father and I baked the
cake and this program will put the frosting on top, you know?"

When I saw that I wouldn't be able to get out of it and
how important my participation was to my mother, I just
agreed. She went on to being so excited about it. Whatever!

I do clean up nice in a tuxedo and I have the etiquette and all. Wasn't really feeling that, though. But for my moms, I'd be down for anything. Then she hit me with another request.

Touching my shoulder she said, "We only have nine guys and they really want one more. I know you got a friend that you could invite to be a part of the program."

"How much is this going to cost, Ma? You know my friends can't afford this extra stuff."

"Boy, you gotta couple of friends whose parents would pay a thousand dollars for this caliber of grooming. Work it out. First meeting is tomorrow and you'll only have to go once a month until you guys are presented in April."

Later that day, I was with Cole and Damarius. As unpolished as they were acting, sitting out the window, yelling out at girls and gobbling down Mickey D's as if they'd not eaten in days, I realized they needed some fine-tuning. My buddies were embarrassing.

"I don't even know why I asked you two turkeys," I said as they joked on me when I mentioned it as we balled in my backyard.

"Tea and an opera concert—stuff like that? Oh, no, man! You got the wrong brothers if you think we'd be interested in that up-under-the-collar junk," Damarius said.

I laughed back. "See, that's what's wrong with y'all fools. You need to expand your horizon. Get cultured!"

"Then you can learn for us," Cole said, "and teach it to us. That way we know everything we need to know without having to take the course ourselves."

"So, you trying to cut corners, huh?" I asked as I dribbled and Cole stole the ball.

"Looks like I'm gonna school you on a few things . . . like this shot! Shhhhh." Cole missed. Damarius and I both laughed.

"Naw, it's cool because I wouldn't want y'all in there embarrassing me and making my moms look all bad."

"Why don't you ask your smart friend? He always trying to hang around you, anyway," Damarius said, actually having a good idea.

"Boy, that's the smartest thing you ever said. Great idea. But now let me school youuu! Nothing but net," I said as my ball went in perfectly.

"Whatever."

Early that evening, I was on the phone with Justin.

"Aww, man, that sounds real cool, but why did you ask me to do it?"

"Actually, it was Damarius's idea. He thought you and I bonding this way would be fun."

Shoot! I didn't know what to say. I mean, he wasn't my first or second choice, but my mom needed somebody else. This was right up his alley. I couldn't believe I didn't think about him first.

Justin's mom talked to my mom and the next thing I know we was sitting next to each other waiting on some late man. I didn't know none of the other brothers that were signed up for this gig. When the late dude arrived, I could've choked on the water I was sipping. To my surprise, it was Saxon Lee.

My mom walked up behind me and said, "Oh, yeah. His mom and I are Links sisters together, though his mom is an AKA, she wants him to be presented to society like his sister will be. Now you won't be the only big athlete in this program."

Saxon didn't even acknowledge me, which was cool. I ain't wanna speak to the brotha no way. Justin saw us looking at each other in a cold way.

"Who is that? You know him?" Justin questioned.

"This football player from South Carolina who thinks he's all that."

Justin joked, "Oh, I thought *you* were, Perry Skky."

"Ha, ha, ha. Very funny!" I said to my friend as I punched him in the arm. "Trust me, my ego's nothing like that jerk."

We learned that each of our five main sessions would be given by a local fraternity, first up was Kappa Alpha Psi, the Nupes, as they called themselves, wearing crimson and cream. They were teaching us about goal setting.

Mr. King took the mic and said, "How many of you know what you wanna be when you grow up?" Only Saxon raised his hand. Why wasn't I surprised? "Yes, young man, tell me your name."

"My name's Saxon Lee, and I know I'm gonna be a pro football player. I'm already on track for that. Best-rated player in the state of South Carolina right now. On course to set records for my high school and the state. I'm being highly recruited, and I will be able to choose my own college. I plan to play for three years, come out early and be in the pros before I'm twenty-one."

"Wow. You'll need some training to set those goals. We have another football player in here, I think, from the state of Georgia, my state. He here?" Mr. King asked.

I raised my hand slightly and nodded my head.

Mr. King asked, "So, do you share his same vision? You wanna play in the NFL, too, I'm sure."

"That's an option, sir. I don't know at this time."

"The rest of you in this room are unsure about what you want to be when you grow up? I want to challenge you. It's great when brothers have a dream. Something that we can work toward. Most of us don't do that. Sports seems like a road that sets brothers on a course to where they hope to go." A lot of us were nodding our heads. "But, Mr. Lee, I sug-

gest you also choose another course of action. Getting in the
NFL or NBA has many odds stacked against you. If you don't
make it, what else are you doing to prepare for another
dream? Make sure you choose a major in school so you will
have something to fall back on. You could get hurt, you could
get injured or you may not be as good in college. Now, I'm
not saying that any of these will happen, but a good man is
always prepared and has another plan in case his first one
didn't pan out. And a great man is able to adjust midstream,
and have a bright future regardless of whether it works out
his way. But to all of you, it's okay if you don't know where
you wanna go. We just need to work on it."

Mr. King told us to start thinking about some of our strengths,
start thinking about careers that interest us and start spending time talking to folks we knew who are already in those
jobs. Sort of interviewing them to see if it was something that
we would like to do. We talked about setting realistic time-
frames, sticking to small goals to actually achieve the big
ones. I really learned a lot from this session. I hated to give it
to my moms, but one thing I came away with from the Goal-
Setting Workshop was that in order to achieve anything, you
gotta see something, and then set steps to actually achieve it.

Though I didn't know what my life purpose was yet, I left
that meeting knowing I would make it my business to find
out so that I wouldn't spend my years doing something that
wouldn't bring me to my goal. But that I would be making
every day, every moment and every step count toward the
bigger goal I was trying to achieve. Yeah. Being a Beaux
seemed like it would be okay after all.

In the locker room, I could not have felt any worse. We'd
just lost our first game of the season. The score was 17-14.
We had the chance to win. We were on the 2-yard line, first
and two, with thirty-two seconds left. Coach had called a

timeout and set a plan to put the ball in my hands. Most coaches' plays indicate that in that situation you run.

Coach Robinson chose to give it to me, and I dropped the ball. That would've been okay 'cause we still had time. However, the defending player from North Augusta caught the ball in the air. It was an interception. They won because of my mistake.

Choked up, I placed a towel over my head in the locker room and just let out what I was feeling.

Damarius came up to me and said, "Aye, man. I let a long pass go when we had them 10-14 and the boy ran sixty yards down the field and scored. I know how you feel. It'll be all right."

The kicker came up to me weeping as well. Saying that he had lost the game for us. Said that there were two field goals he's missed. "I shouldn't have missed those field goals, Perry. They were easy shots, and I missed them both. Those six points are the difference in the game. It's not your fault."

Coach Robinson made his way over to me. "Perry, son, take the towel off your head. Come on in my office so we can talk."

I wasn't moving, though. All this was too hard to bear. To a lot of people, it was just a football game. But to me, missing that ball, letting it slip through my hands like that, losing the game for my team made me realize that football was more than a game to me. I had pride in what I do, and passion when I do it. It was a game I loved. And I loved playing for those guys. I loved winning for those guys. I loved that the coach believed in me enough to put the ball in my hands. Why'd I have to mess up?

No, I couldn't move at that moment when Coach Robinson wanted to say whatever he had to. I didn't know what he was planning to say to cheer me up, but I didn't wanna hear it. There was nothing that could be said.

"I should've ran it," my coach told me, leaning down real close to my towel so that everyone in the whole locker room couldn't hear.

That confession was only for me. I still didn't take the towel off my head. I felt him touch me on the shoulder, hit my locker and walk away.

Much later I came on out of the locker room and into the crowd.

My dad walked up to me and said, "Son, if it wasn't for you and your earlier catches they wouldn't even have been in the position to win tonight. We'll talk about the rest of this when we get home."

The news media wanted to ask me questions, but dad walked me past them and got me to my car. He took my keys from my limp hand and drove me home.

"Son, Cole came up to me and told me how broken up you were in the locker room. Now, I wanna tell you a couple of things here. You gon' be playing with the big dogs in college next year. When you're a superstar player, you're gonna have criticism. You will have more accolades; however, when you gamble with football, you can get burned. But you can't wear your emotions on your sleeve. You can't let people see you cry and be sad. Not your teammates, man. They look up to you for leadership."

My dad went on to fuss about the coach's play calling and time management. Though the coach did admit to me personally he made wrong calls and the players admitted they thought they lost the game, I wasn't about passing blame. I had it in my hands. Nine out of ten times, I would've caught the sucker. But that was the one time when I dropped it and the defender was there to catch it.

This was taking away our hopes for a national championship. That was probably why this loss hurt so bad. Now, we were gonna need some help from other schools to lose, too. You never want to count on anything like that and I'd messed that up for my team.

Though my dad was talking through the rest of the drive home, I wasn't listening. When I finally got home, my mom was waiting at the door with wide-open arms. I just fell into them with red eyes, wishing that I was her little boy again so I wouldn't have to deal with big-boy problems.

"What I tell you, Son? You gotta shake it off. You gotta get tough. I guess the one good thing about this is that it's showing you how much you care about football."

Later that night, I couldn't sleep much.

The next day I couldn't get away from it, either: replays on the local news, newspaper articles, my teammates calling. I couldn't understand why God would let something like that happen. I was a good guy.

Driving around all that Sunday, I couldn't believe where I ended up: at church. I saw Pastor Monroe out by his car, and I turned into the parking lot right beside him.

"Hey, son. I heard you had a rough game last night. Sorry about that," my pastor said as he opened my car door.

I stepped out and said, "I guess the world knows."

"And by the look in your bloodshot eyes, you're not dealing with it well."

"It's not like I'm some big Christian or anything, Pastor Monroe, but I have been talking to God more lately. I honestly don't understand why He would allow me to blow the big game. I thought He was blessing me by setting me up to be the hero, and I turned out to be the zero. What does He want from me?"

"He wants you to do just what you're doing now."

"He wants me to be angry and bitter?" I asked.

"No. He wants you to come to Him with your cares, problems and concerns. He wants you to bring your all to Him. God can do anything but fail, Perry."

"Pastor Monroe, if that's true, then how come He failed me last night?"

"Because you lost the game last night, you think God failed you? Son, you are the most sought-after player in the state of Georgia and as far as football is concerned, you have such a big platform there. God could be using this moment in your life to win more souls for Him. You say you've been talking to the Lord a lot, but you gotta give a little bit more. You've got to read His Word for yourself and see what He really expects from us. I'm not saying he doesn't care about football, but everything is supposed to be done to His glory. Just remember God loves you, son, and He cares about all the things you care about. But more than any of the things in your heart, He wants your desire to be for Him. Only then are you truly pleasing Him and seeking true purpose."

~ 7 ~

Hearing I'm Great

Yes! Things are finally turning around, I thought to myself as I waved good-bye to my mom. We were at the Augusta airport. I was on my way to Miami via Atlanta. It would be my first recruiting visit unaccompanied by my parents.

Sitting in first class, I knew this had to be the life. The seats were wider, and every few minutes the stewardess was coming to ask me if I wanted something else. When I got off the plane and walked to Baggage Claim, I spotted a big sign. It was actually a big jersey that had my number on it. It also said "Skky" on the back of the jersey. All I could do was smile. I saw two other guys waving me down, standing with a man dressed in orange and green. The coach introduced himself first.

He reached for my hand and said, "Coach Sambo Nick, offensive coordinator for University of Miami. We talked on the phone. It's good to have all three of you guys here."

"Thank you, sir," I said, as I saw the other two dudes peeping me out.

"Wow, you're a tall joker," this dude with dreads and huge hands said to me.

Automatically, I slapped hands with the guy that was talking. He introduced himself as Deuce Malet, Florida's top quarterback from Jacksonville. Beside him was a guy with gold teeth. I was glad my mom didn't come. She was so conservative and wouldn't have liked all that gold shining in this guy's mouth. Shoot, she'd probably kill me if she caught me wearin' a grill. Homeboy looked cool, though. He introduced himself as Pony Boy Jones.

"Yeah, my boy back home was telling me about you. He's a DB. Says you the man on defense," I explained.

"What's his name? I might know him, too," Pony Boy told me.

I laughed, "Naw, naw, he's not on your level. You probably don't know his name. He knows yours, though. Twenty interceptions last year and you're already on pace to break that. You're from Tampa, right?"

Pony Boy nodded.

Coach Nick said, "Perry, your plane was the last one to arrive. Now that I've got my recruits, let us be on our way. I'll show you some of Miami."

Soon as we stepped outside, the rain was awful. We didn't have far to walk. We headed straight over to the Hummer limousine. The orange car was stretched pretty.

"We ridin' in style," Pony Boy said.

Deuce got in the car next. I looked back at Coach and motioned for him to go on, but he wouldn't move until I got in. The offensive coordinator was serving us. It was nice to feel really wanted.

Though it was raining, we were driven straight to their stadium. The three of us got on the elevator with the coach and we went up to a suite. A massive spread of food was set out. Coach introduced us to a defensive position coach, a few hostesses and a secretary. Everyone was off the chain nice.

We watched highlights of Miami and then they incorporated something so dope, I would never forget it. Miami was losing to their in-state and conference rival, the Florida State

Seminoles, on the tape we were watching. All of a sudden, they transposed Pony Boy making an interception with only one minute left on the clock. Offense came onto the field. Deuce threw a long bomb to me for a touchdown.

We didn't know how they did the virtual reality thing, but the three of us got excited. Miami won the game. It was amazing.

Coach Nick said, "All right, so you boys think this is cool. Well, that doesn't have to be something we created. Sign here, and it can actually happen next year. We play freshman at Miami. Being members of the ACC and being on the coastal side with Virginia Tech and Georgia Tech, we have to take studs players that can make an impact for us right away. If you feel like you're ready to come to school and perform like that taped showed, we're ready to have all three of you guys committed before the end of this weekend."

After we were charged and full, Coach Nick took us on a tour of the facility. Again, it was thundering and lighting everywhere. It felt like a real hurricane was on the horizon. But Coach Nick wasn't the least bit concerned about danger.

When the lighting struck again Coach stopped moving and said, "Around here we believe that when a severe storm comes any time we have recruits, that is just the Earth's way of saying, '*Sign those guys.*'"

Coach pointed at me. Then he pointed at Deuce. Lastly, he pointed at Pony Boy. Three black boys from three different parts of the South in front of the white offensive coordinator who was looking at us as if we were the best things he'd ever seen in his life. He gave us a vibe like he just had to sign us. I knew I was good, but looking in his eyes and seeing the way he talked so passionately about us coming to Miami made me think I was great.

He then took us to a room where they had pictures posted of all the former Miami players who were now playing in the pros. He left us alone for a second to take a call from the head coach.

Pony Boy spoke first. As his eyes glistened he said, "To be honest, I was thinking about signing with Florida State, but they're making it hard for a brotha. Look at this wall. All these dudes playin' now in the NFL."

"Ah, come on, man," Deuce reminded him, "Florida State's got a lot of players that's on the next level, too now."

"I know, I know, but I've been on a ton of recruiting trips and one was Florida State. No one has roasted me like this yet. I heard they got a big party back at the hotel waiting on us. They gon' set it off," Pony Boy responded.

"Y'all ready to sign?" Coach Nick joked as he came back into the room.

We got word it was a Category 2 storm headed our way. So we hurried over to the head coach's mansion to meet him. Because of the weather, we didn't stay long. He just told us he'd meet us the next day and to have lots of fun meeting all of his players.

When we got to our hotel, the three of us were sharing a suite. The suite had a living area and a kitchenette but there were three bedrooms. We went up to the penthouse, which overlooked the water. Coach Nick told us there were plenty of Miami tapes we could check out near the DVD player.

Coach Nick said, "Enjoy your night with the players. Don't have too much fun, though. We have an early start in the morning to talk to the school president and to meet the academic advisor."

He wasn't gone five minutes when our door was bumrushed by ten of their starting players, a whole bunch of honeys, a big boom box and snacks. The party was on. Pony Boy was groovin'. Deuce was trying to meet every player. I was just watching the overzealous scene and wondered if I fit in.

"Perry," Pony Boy shouted out, "I'm sold for real now. I'ma have to come to Miami."

It was good, clean fun. I got my groove on stepping to the left and jamming to the right for a bit. Meeting the players was cool. I'd watched some of them on TV for the past four years and meeting them in person was a high point. I tried asking the players how they liked the school academically. Quickly, I found they wanted to relax, not talk about books.

I knew I'd always have respect for the University of Miami football program and I was grateful that they wanted to bring me in. I knew I was only seeing a small representation of what life would be like to sign there. But I realized Miami wasn't my speed. The city had too much other stuff going on that could easily distract me, if you know what I mean. Miami is one big party all the time! Though the program turned out studs in the game of football, I wanted to come away from college being a stud at life. I wasn't quite sure Miami could do that for me because I knew I wasn't strong enough to resist the fun. Although I left the weekend not committing either way, I was pretty sure I wouldn't be back that far South.

It was report card day and a lot of the players were either happy or sad. We were dressing out for practice and many were going around comparing grades. I didn't see what the purpose for all that was. The guys should have known what they we're getting before today, anyway. However, there seemed to be a whole lot of disappointed people around me.

Damarious came over to me and whispered, "I need to keep a 2.0 to have a chance of getting to play in college. I got two D's, two C's and one A—in PE—and an F in U.S. history. I'm not making it."

That class was crazy. The subject was not that tough. The textbook said we just need to have an understanding of the three different branches of government. However, our teacher added extras. He wanted us to know names of all the U.S. senators, all the congressman, all the judges, all the president's cabinet members and a few members of the White House staff. He was challenged by some of the parents who were upset about the extra load on us; but the school upheld Mr. Crompwell's decision to stretch our skills.

I remember him saying, "To be really good at U.S. history, you have to go beyond what the books say you need to know."

I didn't particularly care about being good at U.S. history, but I did want to maintain my A, so I buckled down and memorized the material. Looking at my buddy, I knew I had to do something to help.

"Aw, come on D, man," I said as I put my hand on his back, trying to cheer him up. "You can pull up your grades to make your average at the end of the year be a 2.0. Don't sweat this."

"I wish I was more like you. What you got—two A's and some B's? I know them tough AP classes are givin' you a fit."

I tried to step away and place my report card in my locker. I didn't need anyone seeing my grades. We weren't here to compare ourselves.

"What you got, Perry?" Damarius asked again, this time as if he was mad at me. "Hey, y'all. Perry walking around here checking out everybody else's grades. Let's look at his. What you got, a C? Trying to act like my F is all horrible. For you a C is just as bad. Why you ain't showing your report card off?"

"I got it, man!" Cole shouted as he snatched my report card and waved it in the air.

I didn't even want to try to go there with them jokers. This wasn't about me. However, they started chanting, "C, C, C." Where they got that from was beyond me. C's weren't bad. It wasn't my grade, either, though.

Cole looked at the card and said, "Snap. All A's. You the man."

"He got all A's, and he's got them hard classes," a player called out.

I noticed Damarius jet out of the locker room. I got my helmet and jogged after him.

"You didn't have to embarrass me like that," he said as I caught up to him.

"I wasn't tying to show off my report card. It wasn't about any of that. Cole took it. I wasn't trying to let folks know because my grades are my business. Nobody needs to know."

"Yeah, right, your name will be posted in the office on the Principal's List," Damarius said.

"Like anyone reads that." I popped him on his head for acting jealous. "Besides, boy, we need to pull up your grades. What do I need to do, D?"

He turned around and asked, "You'll help me?"

I put my hand on his shoulder, and said, "Anything I can do, you know I will help you."

We hugged. As I lifted my arms, I knew he was my home-boy. I really cared about my friend and I cared about his future. I wanted to do what I could to help him achieve greatness.

My parents were so pleased with how I did on my report card. When it came to my next recruiting visit, they once again allowed me to go by myself. I was headed to Duke University, in Durham, North Carolina.

As we drove from the airport, I had to admit the beautiful scenery grabbed me. This time I was in a minivan with two other recruits. One was Jason Casey from the state of Alabama. He was the best kicker in the South. The other was Mannie Frost. He was a quarterback from North Carolina with curly red hair. The two white boys were friendly but kind of corky. I went to an all-black school, so most of the stuff they were talking about I couldn't really relate to.

So I just rode and gazed at the view from the interstate. I saw a lot of trees and a couple of farms. When we got close to Duke, Durham looked like a small town.

We headed straight to the campus. Where were the brothers? I wondered. Duke had a big football game that day, against their rival school, the University of North Carolina. Though the school was nice and academically top-notch, I had to admit I saw no fire and passion among the players on either team. If this had been a basketball game, these would be the two schools to go to. Duke and UNC were arguably the best in the country. Problem was, it wasn't basketball that I was trying to get a scholarship for.

The game itself was brutal for the spectators to watch. Both Chapel Hill and Duke played horribly that game. Special teams couldn't cover anybody, and neither team got good field position, or could even score. The kicker for Duke missed three that day, and that made Jason Casey, sitting beside me, so excited. He knew that he could make a difference at the school right away.

Their quarterback also got sacked four times in the game, fumbled the ball twice, completed only six passes out of forty and had a pick. He gave a pitiful performance. Mannie Frost was also very elated and ready to commit. I had seen Mannie on tape and he had a good arm. Honestly, I could imagine him throwing the ball to me and making some different things happen.

Duke wasn't appealing to me. I had no clue what I was looking for, but at Duke I wasn't finding it. The pace was way too slow. And for some that might be a good thing, but for me I needed a little bit more excitement.

When the game was over, and Duke lost by ten, we just sat around waiting for dinnertime. I wasn't going to be rude or anything, and tell the people, heck, no, I didn't want to play at their school. I had to keep my options open. Every school in the ACC was top-notch. At Duke, I could certainly get a great education and that couldn't be dismissed by any means. But I did have more in my heart for competing, and I just didn't see them quite there yet. I didn't have to play for the best school in the ACC where football was concerned, but I didn't want to play for the worst, either. Duke needed more help than I could give them.

Later I was sitting in the coach's office waiting for him to finish with the press and come talk to me. His secretary said I could use the phone to pass some time. So I pulled out my cell and thought about calling a number of people. I was actually surprised at the number I dialed.

When the sweet voice of Savoy Lee answered, I was glad.

"I didn't think you'd ever call. I come to your birthday party and you can't even say thank you to a girl," she teased.

"So you know it's me?" I was happy to hear her excitement.

"Yeah, your number popped right up into my phone. How you doing?"

"Cool, I'm on a recruiting visit."

"Yeah, my brother is, too. Where are you? Are you guys together this time?"

"Well, I'm at Duke."

She chuckled, "Duke, no, he's definitely not there. Sax is at Florida State."

"I was at Miami last week," I bragged, which was really weird, because I'd never bragged around Savoy. I didn't want her to think that her brother was so much better than me. So I defended my schedule.

She eased my mind. "It's okay, Perry. I know you're just as good as he is . . . if not better."

"What did you say?" I asked.

"Nope, I'm not saying it again. You heard me, but I don't want you to use it against me when you see my brother next time, or I'll have to deny it." Her spunk was so enticing.

I said, "Naw, Lee got skills."

"Mr. Modest, you do, too. I have seen some of your recent games."

"You have?"

"Yeah, Sax has your tapes. He studies everybody. And some of the catches you make, like the one a couple of weeks ago where you dived over and then missed that last grab. You came closer than anyone has ever seen to making a catch like that. I just hated the game ended like that. "How are you holding up from it?"

"I'm straight. I mean, it happens sometimes, right?" I had to be tough.

"Perry, you can talk to me," she pried. "You okay? The camera showed you on the sidelines after the game, and you were broken."

I laughed about my painful moment and said, "I was, but I can only admit that to you. Don't you tell nobody, or I'll have to deny that one."

"It was just one play. You've shown plenty of moves for schools. For real, stay up," she encouraged.

I heard people talking outside the door. "I think the coach is coming back. I just wanted to call and say hey."

"Glad you did. Where do you go next?"

"Georgia Tech, I think."

"Oh, so is Saxon. That's actually the school I want to go to."

"You . . . you coming?" I hesitated, wanting the answer to be yes.

"I don't want to tie up my weekends like that again. I'm

just thinking about Tech. I want to be an architect, and it's a great school. Handle your business. We'll talk soon."

When Duke's head coach came in, I wasn't even thinking about most of the stuff he said. Though I was very respectful and truly appreciative, it didn't click for me. However, when I got on the plane and headed home, I couldn't help thinking about next week. I asked myself, *Hmm, would it be great to go to the same school with her or would that be asking for trouble?*

"Junior, honey, come here. This is so great!" I heard my mom shout from the kitchen.

I dashed downstairs, full of excitement as well. She didn't get pumped up for much, but since she was calling me, something big had to be going on. "Yes, ma'am?"

"It's your SAT scores. Check this out."

I took the sheet from her and saw that I had made a 2160 out of a possible 2400. The last time my score was lower than that. I was pretty proud of myself to see that I had upped my score. Wow! Hard work was paying off.

"Baby, you can sign anywhere now. I'm so proud of you."

When my dad came in from raking leaves, I saw something between them I hadn't seen in a while. They shared a moment of happiness and joy after my mom rushed up to him and showed him my scores. He gave me a thumbs up.

My mom said, "Our son is awesome."

I couldn't help but laugh. They danced around like kids. He came up and slapped me with a cool high-five.

"I knew you could do it, Son. I knew you could beat your old score. I bet if you took it again you'd get a perfect 2400.

My dad got cleaned up and took us out to dinner. It was amazing, things were going so well for our family.

Dinner was awesome. My parents were getting along,

laughing about things that happened on my two recent recruiting trips. They were both impressed with my reasons as to why neither Duke nor Miami were right for me.

If I could have frozen that moment and kept it forever, I would have. Since life changes so quickly, I took the time after dinner to silently pray and thank God for all that He had done:

> *Lord, a couple weeks ago I was crazy, so upset that I didn't win the big game. As I now see, You can work all things for my good. The school thing is working out. I don't have any doubts, You'll place me where I need to go. I'm also thankful for my parents. I was worried about their relationship, but looking at them enjoying each other is a good feeling. I want to talk to You more. Help me learn how to do that. In Jesus's name, Amen.*

Later that week my folks and I were at Georgia Tech for the big showdown battle of the Techs. The state school was playing Virginia Tech, another ACC rival. Virginia Tech had beaten Georgia Tech the last three or four years. But with this being a home game for Georgia Tech and both teams needing to win it, this was an exciting game for a recruiting visit.

I love Georgia Tech's Bobby Dodd Stadium. It was cozy and not so overwhelming, like some schools I'd gone to. But it was still massive and very appealing to the eye simultaneously. The head coach's office, like in South Carolina, was right inside the stadium. They had just renovated and added on to their stadium. However, I had to admit I was disappointed when I came to my seat right at kickoff and still noticed that there were empty places. The stadium held only fifty-five thousand, but a lot of seats were open. Even at Duke that wasn't the picture. Did I want to play at a place where the fans weren't totally behind the team? Maybe I could be a part of a recruiting class that changed that. Who knew?

Before kickoff, though, Lance Shadrach and Saxon Lee came and sat beside me.

"Wasup, fellas?" I asked, greeting them both.

"They got two senior receivers on the field and a senior QB. I hear their backups in all positions can't touch us. What's up is, are we gonna sign here?" Saxon asked.

"Be careful, Lee, our sisters go to Georgia," Lance said as he tapped my back.

"Like we care about going to school with our sisters," Lance said, like he knew everything.

"Lance, I hear y'all still undefeated," I said.

"Yeah, I might have to lose one so I meet y'all at the state playoffs," he joked back to me.

"I'm just messing with y'all. I'm not ready to commit any-where, either," Saxon said. "Too many folks want me on their team. However, Perry, this is the only school where they need two receivers badly."

"I hear ya, Saxon."

Tech was making an impressive go at beating Virginia Tech 23-17. We recruits liked it when the schools we came to visit ended up winning. And if seniors were on the field or juniors leaving early to enter the draft were winning for their school, that was even better. They'd really need new players to make that kind of impact.

Later, back in the hotel room, I walked in to find my par-ents arguing. My mom was thinking this was the best place in the world and the only place I needed to go. My dad thought that the academic challenge, though I could handle it, might put me under too much pressure.

"All right, guys, keep it down," I said, coming into the room and hoping to interrupt them.

"Son, what are you thinking about this place?" my mom asked.

"It's cool," I said, really having mixed feelings.

My mother politicked. "I know Lance Shadrach is really thinking about going here. His mom just told me, he's almost a shoe-in. He'll commit before he leaves."

"Well, I don't think any of us are sure at this point."

"You know you can't sign right now. You got to keep all your options open," my dad said.

My mom debated, "Honey, goodness forbid something happens to that boy, and he hurts himself before the season's over. He needs to take this opportunity to sign in a place he knows he will like, and that's in the city of Atlanta. It's not Miami but it's not North Carolina, either. This is a good place right in the middle for this boy. He could have a good education and a nice football career. Not to mention he won't be that far away from us."

"Well, if he goes to Athens, he won't be too far away from us, either," my dad responded.

"So, Dad, am I hearing you say Georgia is where you want me to sign?"

"Why not go to school with your sister? It's all about who you know. Tad is up there. Dakari is up there. But they only have one senior receiver slot. I agree with your mom. Ain't no need in holding out if you pretty much know where you want to go. I guess we need to get you signed early after all."

I wish I knew where I wanted to go. I hadn't even been to Georgia's game yet, but I did like Tech. I just wasn't ready to make a decision. It was just October, and signing day wasn't until February. Why the rush?

The next day we drove back home. I thought about the weekend. Georgia Tech had some pluses that made me truly excited. The major thing was that the team chaplain was a brotha who was off the chain. His love for God was actually pretty contagious. I knew that if I sat around him for a bit, I might become a better man of God. However, the academic advisor sort of scared me. I wasn't going to be able to just major in anything. Being an engineer wasn't my heart's desire. Productive recruiting trips confused my mind even more as to where I wanted to go to school.

When I got sick and tired of my parents arguing, I just said, "Hey, guys, enough. I hear you think I've got the great future. And I'm excited to play college ball somewhere, too, but you guys have got to lay off and let me make this decision."

I hated to be so frank with my folks, but I was tired of people telling me that I was such a good student that I could choose any school. It was just a lot of pressure. The only things I could do to stay sane were to stay prayed up and humble in the midst of hearing I'm great.

~ 8 ~

Dealing with Drama

I should have known something was up when Damarius called me early in the morning and asked if I'd stop by and pick him up for school. Cole lived closer to him and so he usually went with Cole in the morning. After I picked D up and listened to him insisting on buying me breakfast, I was ready and waiting for the other shoe to drop. My boy was tight with his cash, and rightfully so. I was even short on mine these days and would have to make a point at getting a little stash from my pops. Even though I knew D had an ulterior motive, I was ready for a chicken biscuit.

Pulling out of Hardees, I quickly said, "All right, D, so what's up? What you want?"

"No, no I don't want much. I just want to give my buddy a biscuit. Brother can't have you going to school looking all hungry and everything. You did come all this way to pick me up."

"Man, cut the bull. For real. What's up? You're not going to have my car to go out on no date. I ain't going out on no date with no girls. Most of my recruiting trips are over and you can't try to weasel your way on one of them."

"Ah, see, you misreading me. Why I gotta want something?" he said to the window instead of my face.

My friend couldn't even look at me at that point. He just chomped into his biscuit and just kept looking to his right. He was sort of nervous-acting. Real fidgety. Yeah, I knew something was up, and the fact that he didn't come out and ask me told me I really didn't want to know what it was. However, before we both got out of the car for school, he grabbed my arm.

"I just need to talk to you for just a sec."

"Man, we been in the car for twenty minutes. I asked you awhile ago. See, you gonna make me late for class."

Again, Damarius was having a hard time communicating with me. Like he wanted to tell me something and then again he didn't want to tell me.

I grabbed my book bag from the back and opened my door, saying, "You just have to come to me when you got all your thoughts together. No need to rush it. Don't stress. Plus, you know we got this big government test second period."

"Okay. That's what it's about."

"You ain't study, boy!" I said in an angry way as I looked over to him.

"That's just it. Perry, I tried. I studied and all those names, they just jumping around in my head. I mean, the senators and the congressmen and the judges, I can't tell 'em apart."

"Well, what you want me to do at this point? I can't cut first period and help you study, man. You ain't gonna get it at that short of notice. If you haven't gotten the material by now, that's a flag."

"I understand. I'm not asking you to skip class to help me."

"Well, what are you asking, D?"

"Remember you told me you'd do anything to help me pull up my grades?"

"Yeah, and I meant that, but not right before the test."

What did my friend think? Did he just think if I drilled him on the names, he'd get it in the last hour? Did he think I was just naturally smart and that's how it came to me? No, I've been studying for a month on all those daggone people. I didn't know what to tell him and I certainly didn't know what he was asking me to do. So I looked at him in a way that was like, come on, what? Finally Damarius came out with it.

"I need you to let me look off your paper."

"You on drugs, son," I joked as if it was a commercial.

"Perry, I'm serious."

"I'm serious. That's ridiculous. I don't cheat and you shouldn't ask me to.

"But that's just it. I'm asking. My grade can't take another F. I promise, if you help me through this time, I'll study with you next time and try to get it like you do. But I'm not intelligent like you, man. I can't get it like that. I just need a little extra help on this one. Cut your partner a break. I've been doing well on the field, Perry. Showing out like you sort of told me to, but if I don't get my grades up, no school is even going to offer me to be a water boy. You know what I'm saying."

Although what he said was hilarious, I could not afford to laugh, 'cause what he was asking me to do was real deep. As I looked at him with his head down, he started getting all emotional, and I knew that he was not playing. What would be the big deal? I mean, he sits behind me. I could just slide my test over a bit. Let him copy off my paper. That's him in the wrong copying, not me. I remembered the time a year ago when Jo-Jo Brown picked me up with a gun. Damarius was his childhood buddy and talked him out of beating my tail worse. He risked it all for me. What kind of a friend would I be if I didn't do the same? I looked at him and though it hurt me to say it, I gave in.

"I'll hold my paper to the side and you can copy off of it."

I quickly got out of the car and shut the door. I was heated. I wasn't happy at all with what I had just told Damarius. And he knew it. I watched him as he walked his usual jovial walk to class, and I felt like I had just conspired to commit a crime. Though I knew it would be hard to live with myself, it would be even harder for me to live without my friend. However, all first period, I couldn't concentrate on school.

When we got into Mr. Banks's class for second period and he handed out the test and roamed up and down the aisle, I thought it would be a little harder than I expected to actually let Damarius see over my shoulder. The test was a breeze for me. All of a sudden I heard a whisper.

"Psst! Perry. Slide it over to the right, man. Banks stepped out."

Without thinking, I followed his instruction. I turned the three-page test to page one, slid all the way over to my right, moved my elbow and body as far as I could to the left, leaving my paper totally exposed for copying.

Thirty seconds later, Damarius anxiously whispered. "Next page, next page."

I listened to how rushed his words were and how quickly his pencil scratched as he wrote the answers. It seemed that my brother had done this before, because I could not understand how he could write down my answers so quickly. Sitting there pondering how much he may have done this, I put my head down. In a matter of seconds, I heard another whisper.

"Last page!"

And right after he said that, Mr. Banks walked over to the both of us.

"You two. In the hallway."

I wasn't the perfect child, but I hadn't cheated in my life. I didn't know what a sick knot feeling was until that day. The knot tugged in my stomach as Mr. Banks walked us to the office. He didn't mind giving us a lecture.

"You know, boys, I'm just so glad I walked in when I did catching you two cheating. See, you athletes think y'all should get through the system any old kind of way. That's why our black boys are always in jail or wind up dead. Thinking they can cheat their way through the system. Not in my class and not on my watch. There will be consequences for you both."

Damarius was steady, trying to weasel his way out of it, saying he wasn't doing nothing and saying Mr. Banks misunderstood. In my mind, why fight what was obvious? If someone asked me, I wasn't going to deny it. I was a lot of things, but a liar—oh, no. Mr. Banks left us in the lobby while he walked into the principal's office and talked to him.

Our principal, Dr. Franklin, was real cool. He'd been at the high school for a long time, even in my sister's day. He would always wear the same black suit. We called him the Black Boss Hogg because on the *Dukes of Hazzard* that little chubby man would wear his black suit, and every day Dr. Franklin didn't fail us. But he was quick to let us know it wasn't the same outfit. Our stay in his office wasn't long at all. As soon as Mr. Banks left, Dr. Franklin spoke with us.

"All right, I'm just going to be frank with you boys. You know I'm a big football knack. Perry here is the best football player in the state of Georgia and getting suspended would ruin a lot things for him, and if both of you get suspended it would ruin a lot of things for me because then we would have less of a chance to win the state championship. So I'm telling y'all what I'm going to do. Mr. Banks is going to give both of you guys an F on this test."

"I can't afford an F," Damarius pleaded.

"You can't afford an F *and* to be suspended. I'm going to lift one of them. Don't push it, now. Study next time, boy," he said as he took a notepad from his desk and whacked Damarius across the head in a playful way. He then looked at me and shook his head. "And, negro, the next time one of your partners asks you to do something shady, stand up, be a daggone man and say no. Do what's right," he said, whacking me in the head next. "In addition to this warning I'm giving you brothers, I will be calling your parents. How much have you learned from this?"

I finally opened my mouth at this time. "I appreciate this. But, umm, do you have to call my folks? I mean, can we work this out?"

"Uh-uh, you all decided to break the rules and now you gonna suffer the consequences."

It was my turn to hold my head down at that moment. Mr. Franklin telling my parents was not good. Guess I'd brought it on myself, though.

My mom was waiting for me when I got home that day and it was not with an afternoon snack.

"Have a seat, Son," she said as soon as I hit the door.

"Mom, I know what you are gonna say and I feel bad about it. D was just up against the wall and needed my help. It was stupid and I won't do it again. Dr. Franklin took care of it. Can we just drop it?"

"No, we're not gonna just drop it. Sit down!" she said forcefully.

I loved my mom with all my heart and it made me feel worse knowing that I had let her down. But, shoot, I wasn't perfect, I was just a teenager. At least there was a type of principle I was standing on behind my decision.

I wanted to help out my friend. I said I was sorry. I said I wouldn't do it again. Why in the world did she feel like she had to drill me on it?

"I see you over there rolling your eyes, boy, like I don't need to say anything to you. Your dad doesn't even know yet."

"Like he's gonna care," I muttered.

"Whether he cares or not, I care. And I got real problems with my son cheating in school. Just when I'm proud of you, thinking your tail is smart, you go and do something so dumb that I just want to disown you. Come on, Junior, what were you thinking? You know some of those teachers are there just waiting for you to fail. You may think you're the best thing since sliced bread, but some people out here I'm sure are haters and think you are a three-month-old loaf ready to be thrown out with the trash. And if they could they'd be the person that takes you to the Dumpster. At the parent-teacher conference, Mr. Banks never says anything good about you, yet you have all A's in his class. Even I know he isn't your fan. And that's the class that you pick to cheat in. Not that you should cheat in any of your classes, but you know the man is on you."

"I know, Mom, and I didn't set out to cheat or do anything like that, but my buddy asked me to help. I helped him. I said it was wrong. What else do you want me to say?"

"I want you to say that you get it and that you understand that it wasn't about you letting me down and letting your dad down—because he does care, despite what you may think—but that it was a test of your character and about not letting yourself down even when you are trying to humbly help a friend. Start doing some things, Son, and it just might become a habit."

"Mom, I don't plan to keep cheating."

"No, but you didn't plan on cheating today, either. That's my point. I don't want you to do things that you know are wrong because you may not know when you can stop and go back to doing what's right. I just want you to make wise choices and until you do, you are grounded. After those ball games, bring yourself into this house."

"Mom!"

"You think about what I said. I got to get up early in the morning and clean. I really don't have time for this, Perry. Just-Just go."

The next day was more of the same. My mom was on me seriously this time. I was tired of her ranting. So when she stepped to me I said, "Moms, I got it. I'm not leaving the house. I'm just going out in the backyard to shoot some hoops. I just want to stay in shape. Is that cool?"

"No, it's not cool when I found this in the bathroom." She held up an unopened gold, square wrapper.

Ah, snap, I thought, looking at the condom she held firmly in her hand.

"It's just protection, Mom." I laughed as if that was a dumb question to ask me.

"Don't get smart with me, boy. I know what it is. Why in the heck do you have it? Who you trying to get with? I know Tori is a virgin. You and I talked about messing with that sweet, innocent girl."

"Mom, I hate to break it to you. I'm eighteen. I'm not no little boy anymore. How long do you think I'm supposed to stay a virgin?"

"Let's start with til you married. Is that a good answer?"

"It ain't realistic. If that's all you have to say about this, then we don't even really need to be talking about this. I'm sorry I left it out and that you saw the thing."

"Wait a minute, boy! You don't talk to me like you done lost your mind."

"I'm sorry, Mom. I not trying to disrespect you. It's just that you living in a world that's not reality. You think I think it's cute that I haven't had sex yet and I'm suppose to jump all up and down and be all excited that my mom is proud of me still being pure. Oh, Mom, let me live my own life and you just work on yours," I said as I snatched the condom out of her hand, put it in my sock, and headed out back.

The rest of the day passed quickly. My mom didn't talk to me and I didn't talk to her. She was probably flabbergasted by how I came off. I had left her speechless. No words did I want to take back, though.

Later on that night, around 11:45 PM, I got the munchies. I headed for the kitchen to fix me a bowl of Frosted Flakes. A large bowl at that, with lots of milk. Even though I wanted to eat, I was sidetracked. I heard something coming from the living room. Peeping in there 'cause I was sort of afraid that it might be an intruder, I was shocked to find my mom there crying. *Whoa,* I thought to myself. I knew I meant what I said to her earlier, but did I have to be so harsh as to make her cry?

"Moms," I said, falling to her knees. "I'm sorry."

"Sweetheart, this doesn't have anything to do with you. I didn't want you to see me like this. I know you're not going to stay a baby forever. I know it. I just worry about you. Diseases and getting girls pregnant."

"Mom, I know about all that stuff. If it's not about me, then what is it about? What's wrong with you?"

"Son, I don't want to talk about it. Just go to bed. What are you doing up, anyway?"

"I was hungry."

"Let me get up and fix you something."

"No, no, mom. I was just going to get some cereal. I do that a lot when you and Dad are asleep. Where is he? Does he know you're up? Let me go get him. Did he do something to you?"

Before I could leave the room, she grabbed my arm. "No,

your dad is not here. Again. Just stay out of it. Don't be concerned about me, okay?"

"Mom, did he hurt you? Did he hit you?"

"No, Junior. You know your dad is not violent. It's nothing physical and plus I just said all I can about this to you."

I too couldn't believe that I had to ask my mom did my dad hit her, but after what I saw a month ago, it was still engraved into my mind. I had to make sure. She gave me a kiss on the cheek. At that moment, I wasn't hungry anymore. That knotted feeling was in my stomach again. However, I got the big bowl of cereal, anyway. The milk tasted sour and the flakes were stale. I poured the whole bowl out. Drama!

The next day was Sunday, and everyone was ready to stay out late. Since we didn't have school on Monday because of Columbus Day, a lot of folks headed to the local skating rink for a fall jam. I decided to swing through there. Thankfully, my mom had forgotten all about my punishment. She had her own issues. So when she said I could head out and not to worry about her, I took off. I started to go alone, but then I thought about Tori. I wanted to be with my girl.

I really was trying not to focus on sex, but a big part of me wanted it. I wanted Tori. A big part of me wanted this to be our night, so I packed a cooler full of root beer, brought a bag of her favorite guacamole chips and headed over to her house. My goal was to surprise her and take her someplace special to get the night going.

Her pretty brown face greeted me. "Hey!" she said, excited to see me.

"Is it all right if I come in? I know I didn't call. I was just trying to surprise you," I said, pulling flowers from behind my back.

"Sweetie, these are so nice. Yes, thank you, come in. My mom's upstairs. It's cool."

"I was coming by to see if you wanted to hang out and go to the skating rink with me. I have a fun evening planned for the two of us, can you go get ready?"

"Ooh!" I heard a little voice say, "Tori's boyfriend is here."

Tori pointed to the little girl watching us from around the corner. "I would, but I'm baby-sitting."

It was just my luck. My girl had to spend her night watching a kid. I had to think of another plan.

"Can't your mama do it or something? You said she is here."

She placed her hand on her hip and said boldly, "I'm getting paid to watch her. I can't just push this off on my mom. Besides, I didn't know you were coming over. I hadn't seen you in a couple of weeks. We hadn't even talked, Perry. I've called and left messages, but you haven't returned my calls. I mean, what am I supposed to think? Am I just supposed to keep myself available, hoping, wishing and praying that you'll come by?"

"All right, fine, whatever," I said, real frustrated, turning around to head out the door.

Tori grabbed my hand. "Wait, wait, wait. Lynn, can you put your *Barbie* movie on? I'll be right there, okay?"

"Can I watch it in your room?" she asked, real excited.

"Okay, sure. But don't mess up my bed," Tori replied.

As soon as the little girl left, I grabbed my girlfriend and pinned her up against her front door. The passion from my body went through my lips to hers. I wanted her to feel how badly I wanted her in so many ways. Wanting her to feel so many things, wanting her to want to be with me badly. She started returning my advances, grabbing my bottom. That made the distance between us ever so small. She placed her hand on the back of my head and pulled my ear to her mouth.

Tori whispered deliciously, "Baby, I missed you."

Dressed in sweats, Tori was as cute as a baby doll. Truthfully, I was grateful for the baggy pants she had on. It gave me easy access to slide my hand in back of them. I had to get her out the house and into my car. The night needed to be on. I knew my dad's old Luther Vandross CD would make a perfect party for two. She had to come. It was clear she was feeling me.

"You got to come with me, baby. We can't stop this."

"I can't," she said, pulling away from me. "We can't do this."

"What do you mean?" I asked, trying not to be angry.

"We just can't." She opened her front door and pushed me out of it.

"Look, I will be at the skating rink if you change your mind."

"I'm just being honest. I won't be coming."

When she shut the door in my face, I didn't know what to think. Was she trying to stop herself from going further than she wanted to or was she trying to tease me? Either way, I was dying inside.

As I drove to the rink, I started pushing the peddle harder and harder, going faster and faster. Not really caring about the road, a brother needed to let loose. Driving carefree felt good.

When I got inside, Amandi rolled up to me and rubbed against me.

"Perry, you seem tense. I just want to make you feel good."

She looked good in her almost-see-through blouse. She kissed my neck, and I closed my eyes and let the good times roll. I knew she wasn't Tori, but if Tori didn't want to play, why should my fun end?

"Let's go to my car," I told her as I took her arm and headed back outside.

"Sounds good to me. Let me just take my kicks off, baby, and we can have some fun."

As I walked with Amandi, I knew I didn't know much about her. It was clear she didn't have any morals. Always flaunting her body for the whole world to see. Guess she thought guys like it when they didn't have to use their imagination to imagine her goodies.

I wasn't trying to make this chick my girlfriend or anything. Just get my first time over, have some fun and move on. Guess I was about to become everything I hated in my boys.

When I got into my car it wasn't about the music; it wasn't about toasting with the root beer, and it sure wasn't about laughing, talking and all that. This was about a physical attraction only. And as soon as she kissed me, it was on. Amandi was doing a lot of things with me, and they all felt wonderful. Though I did feel like I was doing something wrong, I couldn't stop. My flesh outweighed my spirit. Before we could take it to that final step, though, there was a knock on my window.

Amandi said, "Ignore it. It's not the police or anything."

So I went back to having my fun, never looking up. However, the knock on the window grew stronger. When I reluctantly looked up, I saw Tori's puppy-dog eyes swollen with tears. A sickening feeling welled up in my body. What in the world was I to do next? I was busted. How in the heck was I going to handle dealing with the drama?

~ 9 ~
Breaking Her Heart

As I pulled up my pants, I felt terrible. My eyes were locked with Tori's. And although the foggy glass was between us, I saw the tears streaming down her face. I had crushed her.

She screamed like an insane person. "How could you do this?" Then she dashed away.

I raised my seat all the way up and hit the steering wheel really hard. I never meant for her to catch me. I never meant to devastate her. What was I to do now?

"Our time can't be over," Amandi said as she rubbed on my bare chest.

"I'm looking for my shirt. I-I need to go talk to her. Stop."

"Pssh. Talk to her? You all right? We're in the middle of something. I think she gets the message that y'all are through."

"Look, I'll catch up with you later. I need to speak to her," I said before grabbing my shirt and opening up the car door.

Buttoning my shirt quickly, I jogged, trying to find Tori between the cars. I didn't even think I was gon' find her as I searched through the first two rows. But when I got to the next one, I saw her bent down in the dirt, crying.

"Aww, Tori," I said, trying to pick her up.

But then she started kicking and swinging at me crazily. This situation was way out of hand.

"Let me go! Don't touch me ever again!" she screamed.

"I'm just trying to pick you up. You shouldn't be all on the ground like this. I get it. You're mad at me. You wanna let me have it. Here I am, right here."

"What is it, Perry? What does she have that I don't? Everybody already knows that she is—"

I hated seeing her so messed up. "Don't even do that, Tori. Don't belittle yourself by talking 'bout other people."

"What do you care? You're belittling *yourself* by getting with her."

"We didn't even do nothing," I said, but knowing she wasn't gonna buy what I was selling.

With her hand on her hip she said, "Yeah, that's because I came by and stopped y'all."

All of a sudden, she unzipped her raincoat. Underneath, she was wearing only a fine black teddy. My eyes were stunned.

"I was coming to give myself to you tonight. I was going to tell you let's go drive somewhere. I was ready. How stupid am I? I hate myself. I shouldn't even live!"

Then she took off running. I chased behind her quickly. I was sort of confused by what I heard her say. *Not even live?* Was she talking 'bout killing herself over this? No!

I caught up with her, but she was already in her car. The doors were locked. She sped away, kicking the dirt on me. Full-speed, I jetted back to my ride. I just knew Amandi would be gone, since I'd told her I had to go talk to my girl. But the girl didn't get it. She was in the backseat of my ride—nude.

I did a double take. I couldn't believe what I was seeing. Before me was a guy's dream, yet I knew I couldn't entertain anything else with her. My girl was talking about ending her life. I could only pray she wasn't serious. But I couldn't take any chances. I had to catch up with Tori.

"Amandi, we gotta pick this up another time," I said sensitively, trying not to make another girl lose it.

"You gon' turn all this down?" she asked me. I saw her clothes in my passenger seat and I tossed them to her without turning around. "I don't mind if you look," she said.

"Come on, now. I gotta go. I told you that."

"Go! Tori is the one that needs to go now. I don't know why you like her, anyway," she said as she leaned up behind my seat and placed her hands on my head. "She's just a junior, Perry."

"What does her grade level got to do with this? Please, put on your clothes. I'm serious. This is not good. She's real upset, and I'm worried about her. I'll call you."

I heard her grunting angrily from behind my seat as she twisted and turned her body in all kinds of directions to try and straighten her tight skirt and tiny blouse. I felt bad. Now I had two girls to deal with.

"Okay, you gotta get out the driver's seat so I can leave your little car," she snapped.

When I stood up to let her out, she motioned for my hand to help her. I ain't have no problem with being a gentleman, but I was in a hurry. I yanked her a little hard.

"Darn," she said as she fell into my arms purposefully.

Then she kissed my neck and made her way to my lips. What did she think, I was gonna change my mind?

"All right, Amandi. I gotta go."

"Can't believe you're turning me down! Next time you won't get off so easily. Go see about your lil' girl!"

I threw my hand up to motion bye. I didn't have time to be playing games. I was sorry the night ended the way that it did. I wasn't trying to lead her on. I was serious about wanting to make things happen, but circumstances came and intervened and stopped all that. Right then, I needed to find Tori.

"You gotta get back inside the rink. I don't want you out here alone," I said as Amandi just started hanging by my ride.

"It ain't like you care about me."

"I do, Amandi. Go in there."

As soon as I saw her walk through the door, I drove off. I drove around for twenty minutes trying to find Tori. I was having no luck anywhere. Then I remembered she and I parked sometimes in the new subdivision, Autumn Parc. They had only cut in the roads so far; no house construction had been started. Sure enough, I saw a car in front of me down a cul-de-sac.

As I got closer, I confirmed it was Tori's. I parked my car next to hers. She was inside, her head was back, the windows were locked and her car was running. This was crazy. I banged on her window, but she ignored me. I went over to the other side and banged hard.

"Open up, Tori! This is crazy and I need to talk to you. Tori! Tori!" She wasn't responding. "Don't make me break this window. Tori!"

She opened her car door and fell into my arms. A pill bottle fell out as well. It wasn't empty. It seemed she'd only contemplated taking them. I picked her up and sat her outside. Then I went back and turned off her car.

"Were you thinking about taking these pills, Tori? Huh? Tori, answer me! What were you thinking, Tori?" I asked. She was nonresponsive and real drowsy. "What is going on with you?"

Then she spoke: "No, what's going on with you? For the last few years all I've ever dreamed about was being with you. Giving myself to you in every way. You have no idea how you've hurt me tonight!"

"I feel bad, but you can't do this."

"What have I got to live for now?" she whispered.

I wasn't about to drive off and leave her so emotionally devastated. I held her and listened until she calmed down. One thing never changed, and that was her saying how bad I let her down. How I'd destroyed her world, and how she'd never be the same.

As I followed her home, I could only hope to make things better for her heart somehow. However, knowing she was willing to end it all over me had probably scared me away for good.

The next day I didn't have time to reflect on what had happened. It was mid-October and school had been in session for a couple of months. My boys Damarius and Cole asked me if I wanted to hang out with them at the mall on Columbus Day. I was down with the plans since I needed some new threads. I was actually tired of the same old shirt popping up every other week. I needed to add some variety to my wardrobe with a couple of pieces here and there.

I was nothing like my sister at the mall. She could stay there with my mom all day and night. I knew my boys only wanted to go there to hook up with some girls. Although my eyes might roam, my gaze never holds any real intention behind it. But I'd need some more cash to buy shirts, a pair of kicks, some jeans and some slacks.

Since this semester started off a little rocky with my pops, I never got my full run of funds. I needed to correct that. So I headed to the dealership. He was having his Columbus Day sale, and I knew he'd be slaving away trying to make some things happen.

"Don't let your dad put you to work," Damarius said through the receiver. "We need to hang now, bro, not wash dirty cars and stuff."

I was talking to him on the cell phone and trying to drive at the same time. He was so silly. The boy constantly made me laugh.

"Man, I won't be long. I'ma meet y'all at the mall."

"You coming in through Sears, right?"

"Yep, in thirty."

"All right, slick. Tell your dad to cut me a few dollars, too."

"Oh, now you really got jokes."

Before I stepped out the car, I had to check myself. See, I loved to flirt with my dad's secretary, Clarissa. She'd only been working at the dealership since the beginning of the year. However, she made most of the salesmen not concentrate on selling cars. Yeah, she was fine, and she wore some clothes that would make any customer stay too long in our showroom.

But when I stepped into the showroom, she wasn't at the podium. Phones were ringing off the hook, and I stalled for a minute or two to see if she was coming around the corner or from the bathroom. But that didn't happen. I looked at my watch and saw I didn't have much time to fool around.

I headed up to my dad's office and was surprised to find my dad's office door closed. He always had it open so he could scream down at people. His office windows had blinds and they were all shut. Well, except for one. I went down to that window and peeked in. I was shocked to see my dad and Clarissa locking lips! I knew she was fine and all, but I didn't know my dad thought so, too. Somebody needed to show his married behind how to keep his hands to himself. Guess I was the man for that job. I paced back and forth, trying to figure out what I was going to do.

Talking out loud I said, "I can't believe this!"

What did this mean for my family? He was married to my mom, and he wasn't going to do what he wanted to do. He needed to know I wasn't going to have him disrespecting my moms. I tried to turn the knob, but it was locked. So I banged on the door.

"Dad, I know y'all in there. Dad, open the door!" I shouted loud enough to shake the whole building.

His door flew open, and I caught Clarissa trying to fix herself up. All of a sudden, she was disgusting to me. I actually hated that I ever saw anything in her.

"Umm, Clarissa, that'll be all. I'll talk to my son right now. Thank you."

My father was trying to dismiss the whole thing.

Stepping boldly to him, I said, "Save that mess, please! What's your saying, Pops? 'I was born at night, but not last night?' What you think, I'm stupid or something? No, I'm the guy you're proud of. The straight-A student that scored high on his SAT. Some stuff you can't pull on me."

Clarissa slid by me. I didn't even acknowledge her. When she was gone, I let my dad have it.

"Son, I don't know what it is you think you saw," he said after I told him a thing or two. He went around me and shut his door. "All right, you think you know everything. I'ma lay it out for you. Me and your momma are having some problems, and it don't have nothing to do with you."

"It had everything to do with me when you carelessly left your blinds opened so people could see. How long has this been going on?"

"Ain't nothing going on. I mean, we crossed the line a little, but that's it. The stress level at home is just high, and I was a little vulnerable tonight. But I don't need to explain this to my kid. Stay the heck out of my business and keep your mouth shut!"

I went up to him and grabbed his shirt collar. "You cheat on my mother, and I will never forgive you. She may not be perfect, but she has loved you all these long years with all her heart. And with your actions you're breaking it, and you're breaking my mine, too."

"What did you come up here for, Junior?" my dad asked as he loosened my grip.

"I was going to the mall with my boys."

"Well, here, let me give you a lil' something."

"I don't want your money, Dad."

I walked out of his office knowing I couldn't look at my dad the same again. At least now I knew why I caught my mom crying. I never thought my parents' marriage was really in trouble, but after what I'd just seen, my mom shouldn't have been spending her time crying. She should've been packing. 'Cause she was just too beautiful and too special a lady to let any man, even my dad, treat her wrong.

And as her son, I was going to have to protect her. Some way, I was going to have to figure this out.

It was only Wednesday, and Amandi had called me over a hundred times. Most of her messages said the same thing: *I want to get with you again, Perry*. I just wished she understood how unattractive that was.

My dad told me long ago, *"Son, you never want a girl who takes the chase out of the relationship. You wanna be the man, the pursuing one. Fast girls are fun, but they're the ones that cause you the most trouble. They don't know how to leave you alone, and they end up being too needy."*

I didn't know why I was remembering anything he ever told me. For the last few days, we hadn't talked at all. And I hadn't even been in the same room with my mom. I'd been avoiding her so she wouldn't sense what was on my heart.

When the phone rang again at 11:55 at night, I instinctively grabbed it and said, "Hello."

"I don't understand, Perry. What's up? Why are you avoiding me?" Amandi asked.

The chick was wild! Just talking fast, like ninety minutes an hour, sounding like she had drunk eight cups of coffee or something. Didn't she get it? I wasn't trying to get with her!

"Amandi, look, it's late. We gon' have to talk tomorrow—"

"Don't you hang up on me! I been calling, and you ain't called me back!"

"All right, I'm listening. But I'm sleepy. What you gotta say, Amandi? Huh?"

"You sound like you're agitated with me, Perry. You told me the other night that we'd hook up again, and I was thinking about Friday night after the game."

"But you know I got a girlfriend."

"Friday night after the game, come to my house."

"What? What you sayin'?"

"No, no. My parents gon' be home. My dad's a huge football fan. He's barbecuing, and I know you'll be hungry."

"Your dad still got the grill going in October?"

"Yeah. He works at Hally's BBQ. They got the real thing. Ribs, hash, rice—he wants to hook you up. He's been on me to ask you. So, you gon' do it, or what? Can you come?"

"Sure, whatever. Friday it is," I muttered quickly, happy to finally say whatever to get her off my back.

Thursday in school Amandi saw me two times and reminded me that I had agreed to see her the next evening.

When she came up to me Friday after our win, I scoured the stands looking for Tori. But I didn't see my girlfriend or her pom-poms anywhere.

"So are you following me, or what?" she asked.

"I ain't gon' be able to stay long, Amandi. My parents done set a curfew on me and everything. Plus I got a interview with ESPN early in the morning."

"No problem. My dad just wanna meet you, that's all."

Damarius came up from behind me and hit me in the knee, bending me down and scaring me. "Boy!"

"Oh, what's up, what's up? Your reflexes ain't good?" Damarius teased.

"You gon' make me hurt myself."

"Well, let me stop, then. I ain't got a million dollars to pay for what those knees are worth. So, what's up? You done tapped that?" he asked, as he pointed at Amandi walking away.

"Her?" I questioned, trying to throw him off.

"Look at you wit yo head in the gutter. I'm talkin' 'bout tappin' them books."

"Oh, so now you got jokes?" I hit my boy in the arm. "Want to slide with me over to her crib? I'm just going over there to grab a bite to eat."

"Naw, man, I'm good. I'm finished taking all my 'down there' medicine," Damarius said as he pointed to his zipper. "I was thinking 'bout having a party for myself tonight. Me and Ciara. It's been a long time!"

"You ain't learned nothing?"

"I'm straight for real," he said as we slapped hands before parting.

I followed Amandi to her house. When we pulled up it was pitch-dark. No lights or nothing. It looked like nobody was in the house cooking anything.

Quickly, I jumped out the car. "What's up?"

"I think they're trying to do a surprise thing for you."

"Surprise?"

"You are this town's biggest player."

She wasn't making any sense, and I was so hungry. The whole drive over I couldn't wait to smack on some ribs. When we opened the door, nobody jumped out and said, "Surprise!" She just shut the door, and I couldn't see a thing. She found my lips and started heating up the place.

"Wait a minute, now. Hold up, girl. Ease back. Is your pops here? I ain't tryin' to get no shotgun to me!"

"Don't worry," she said as she grabbed my ear.

I was trying to find the light switch on the wall, but my hand was unsuccessful. Then I pushed her back a little. I was upset.

"Where's the daggone light, girl? I'm hungry. I'm not here for this."

Still slobbering on my ear, she said, "I guess I'ma feed your appetite with this. Just relax and enjoy it. You don't think I brought you all the way out here to eat dinner, did you? This ain't my house. This is my cousin's house. She works at night and is letting me use her place. Instead of being in an old cramped car, we got a bed this time."

"Amandi, look. Turn the light on now. Now!" I said even more forcefully.

She quickly turned on the light. "I don't know why you're tripping. We were just together a week ago, and it was more magical than a ride at Disneyland."

"That's a stretch, Amandi. I was just a brother trying to get his groove on and got caught by my girl. I thought about it and I ain't trying to go there again with you. I'm sorry. I thought you would've got it when you called me all those times, and I didn't return one. Maybe you needed to hear me say it. I ain't trying to do that with you."

Right before my eyes, she started stripping! It was like she heard me say, *"Okay, let's do this."* Of course that is not what I said.

"All right. I'll just see you later 'cause obviously you don't understand."

As I opened the door and left, I heard her slam it right behind me. The situation was getting real crazy. Before I reached my ride she opened up the door and ran toward the car, barely clothed.

"You gon' walk out the door on this? Go ahead and act like a punk! You don't wanna cross me, Perry Skky! You need a second chance 'cause you already let me down once. You don't wanna mess with me!"

"You're right!" I told her. "Now you're getting it. I don't

wanna mess with you," I said sarcastically, knowing she had meant something completely different. I gently pushed her to the side and opened up the car door.

She yelled, "How could you do this to me? I thought you wanted me, Perry. I love you!"

I really had a lot to deal with. Amandi could be so dramatic. The way she was trying to force herself on me made think something was really wrong with her. Uh-uh. I wasn't going out like that my first time.

And it was my fault. I did owe her an apology. I had led her on for a week prior. But I was a different me now, and she needed to respect that and understand that I felt bad for what I'd done to Tori. As bad as I felt about what my dad was doing to my mom. The apple didn't fall too far from the tree, I guess.

When I drove off, I noticed Amandi kneel down and curl up into a ball by her cousin's door. Maybe I had been too rough on her. But I couldn't go back and comfort her because she would get it all wrong. I just had to pray for her and hate that I was breaking her heart.

~ 10 ~

Hearing Tough Stuff

I'd come to the conclusion that understanding females was a stress I did not need. I mean, who could figure them out? They couldn't even figure themselves out most of the time. They were either dealing with cycles, mood swings, temper tantrums or some other form of drama. I figured it was best if I stayed my distance from them for a while. But as hard as I tried to keep away, somehow problems with a female found their way back to me.

Amandi kept trying to reach out to me. It was just annoying. Every time my phone rang, it was Amandi calling with some more junk. Studying for my U.S. government test, I was startled when my phone rang because I thought I put it on silent. Turned out, I had it on high.

"Dang, why she calling again!" I said, agitated that Amandi's number showed up on the screen.

I realized that I might as well talk to her. Looked like me trying to ignore wasn't gon' do anything. She'd just keep calling back. Her actions were close to stalking. What the heck was a brother going to have to do to put some distance between us? I guess the answer was to face her.

So I said in a bland tone, "All right, what's up?"

"I don't get a hello or anything?"

"Naw. I think we way past that. You have been ringing my phone like crazy."

"So, you have gotten my messages?" she asked in a testy way.

"Yeah, but I haven't listened to them. But I do see that you've called."

"So why haven't you called me back?"

"I don't think I owe you those kinds of explanations."

"It's like that now, Perry?"

"Look, I'm not trying to be mean here. We tried, and it didn't work for me. What does a brother have to do to end this thing?"

All of a sudden, I heard this rush of emotion come through the phone. Sorta psychotic and depressed, almost scary. "I thought you loved me," she said through tears.

"Amandi, quit trippin'! You couldn't have thought that. You never heard those words once come out of my mouth."

"It was the way you kissed me that said that."

I replied, "Yeah, right. That was the feeling of a brother trying to get his groove on. Don't make more out of it."

Then she showed me another side of herself. The crying stopped, and she went ballistic. "Fine, then, Perry Skky. You think you're the world's gift of Lucy Laney High School? I'ma take you down!"

"Oh, so you threatening me now?" I asked, without backing down.

She didn't even respond. I just heard a click. So many ungodly names came to my mind for that girl. I just shook my head and left it alone.

I knew some girls didn't take rejection well, but this chick was over-the-top crazy. It was cool that she hung up on me. Wouldn't have to deal with her no more. And that would make hearing her little threat worth it. I mean, what could she do?

When my phone rang an hour later I was so relieved that it wasn't Amandi. And actually it made me smile when I noticed Tori's number.

"Hey!" I said in a real excited tone. "You been all right?"

"Perry, let's cut the fun and games. Don't act like you're all excited to hear from me."

"Wait, but I am," I told her in the most sincere voice I could use.

Tori said, "I just called to let you know that you wouldn't have any obligations to me anymore. I wanted you to know I was okay, and I appreciate you following me home the other night. Since you've moved on, I've decided to move on, too."

I wondered what that really meant. Did she mean move on to date somebody else, move on and try to kill herself again or just simply move on? I didn't know what she'd do with the rest of her life, but I hoped she was excited about having it in front of her.

We both sat on the phone and held it for a minute. I couldn't respond 'cause I really didn't know what I was feeling. Sure, guys like to be the ones that end the relationship, but I didn't wear my emotions on my sleeve like that. I mean, whatever made her happy was cool. She'd finally accepted that we were over. After dragging it on for an hour, and telling her I'd always be there for her, we hung up the phone.

The next day at school, my name was mud. Everyone was whispering as I walked down the hall. I didn't know what I had done, so I played it cool. Finally, Justin came over and nudged me over to follow him.

"Man, what's up?" I asked. "You know what all this is about? Why people staring at me? What's going on? They staring like I just got out of jail or something."

"Naw, man, people ain't looking at you like you into mischief. The word's out that you're scared to have fun."

I jabbed him with the back of my hand. "What do you mean, I'm scared to have fun? Say what you gotta say."

Justin mouthed, *okay*. "Amandi's telling everybody that you wouldn't go there with her. I don't need to fill in the blanks, do I, Perry? Dang, what's up? The word's out you're a virgin."

He grabbed my shoulder like I was in crisis mode or something. I jerked my body away from his grasp, not needing consoling. I walked straight on to class. The snickers and the whispers got louder and louder.

I wish somebody would step to me, I thought to myself as I turned and gave everybody a mean glare.

They was talking 'bout me over to the side in their little cliques and crews, but ain't have no guts to say nothing to my face. I held my head up high and kept moving. But now at least I knew what Amandi meant by threats. She got me that time. I didn't have to acknowledge what was going on. Let people think what they wanna think.

Walking along, I prayed. *"Lord, I know I don't talk to You much, but this just don't seem comfortable, people speaking bad things about me and all. Please help a brother stay strong, that's all. Amen."*

I knew I was going to have to pray more often because nobody's comments or actions got to me anymore that day. It was trip, though! I went on 'bout my business, cracked a few jokes, spoke to people here and there, and was my usual self. When I didn't buy into the mess, life was cool.

A couple of people actually came to me and said that they agreed with my choice. I wasn't going to say I wanted to stay pure, but I did know that ever since I turned my stress over to God, I was mentally able to handle anything that came my way. That was important.

* * *

After practice when I stepped off the football field, Amandi was waiting by the gate. I just kept on walking. Then I felt somebody push me in the back. It was Marlon.

He said, "What's up, Perry? You can't even talk to the chick? Dang, maybe she right. You is scared of her. All of us around, we ain't gon' let her bite you."

It took all the strength I had not to knock his crooked, yellow teeth out. When I noticed how all the football players were checking out my reaction I knew I needed to respond. But Marlon got nothing from me.

I turned to Amandi and said, "You wanted to say something?"

With watery eyes she said, "I just wanna apologize. I know you heard that I had been saying some stuff."

"You talking about the rumors you spreading on me? You think I'm affected by that?"

"I know you're not, baby. I just wanted to get your attention."

"Look, I told you the other night at your cousin's house that we tried it, and it wasn't working for me. But if spreading lies and saying whatever about me makes you feel better, that's on you. Don't think that me hearing this stuff is going to make me wanna get with you again. I had empathy for you when I was at your house, or whoever's house we was at. But right now, I don't care. Take it however you want, but leave me alone."

I walked away, and she was clearly devastated. The guys started laughing around me and that wasn't my intent, either. I wasn't trying to embarrass her, but honestly, it wasn't like I really cared if she was hurt. That's what she gets for trying to play me.

"Man, man, man. You ain't gon' like this," Damarius said as he came up to me before practice the next day.

"What's up, man? What's wrong? Somebody done spread another rumor on me, huh?" I joked.

"It ain't about you, dog. But you will care."

Putting on my cleats, I turned and said, "What you talking about?"

"It's Tori." Damarius paused before saying more. "Word's out she and Marlon . . ."

He didn't even have to say more. The way he looked at me seemed like something naughty was going on between them. I just shook my head, letting him know that I didn't believe that.

"I'm serious, dog. You know I wouldn't come to you with no junk."

I knew Tori told me a couple of days ago that she was moving on but there was no way in the world that she would quickly give up her beliefs for that chump. I kept getting dressed for practice. My boy thought I should be tore up, I guess.

So I said, "Why do people always try to rattle me? Try to get under my skin? Try to make me believe stuff I know is impossible. Last time I checked, two plus two does not equal three. I don't believe what you're saying."

"All right, fine," Damarius said as he grabbed his helmet. "Marlon himself told me, and he was way too explicit with it. He told me he was gon' talk to you about it. I told you because I don't want you to lose it out there on the football field. I mean, we got a big game this weekend and we can't afford to get sidetracked. Our two receivers gotta be in sync."

"I don't catch any balls from him," I said angrily. "And I wish he *would* come to me talking some mess about him and Tori. Might as well get smacked down. Contrary to what anybody thinks, I ain't no punk. I don't have time to play games with him or you. I mean, come on, D! You my buddy, squash some stuff for me. Have my back. Why I gotta handle your business and mine? Can't you pull your own weight some-times?"

After I angrily said those words and opened the locker room door, I wished I could take it back. I wished I hadn't said what I said to my friend. But dang! He liked drama like a female. And I wasn't about all the negativity.

Everybody was warming up on their own. As soon as I squatted down to stretch, Marlon came over, whispering in my left ear. "I could tell you some stuff about Tori that would blow your virgin mind."

It was on then. I took off my shoulder pads and shoved him straight into the ground. I was about to jump on him and pound his nose in so hard that it'd be worse than broken when I was finished with it. But someone stepped in be-tween us.

I was so caught up in the moment that I didn't even know who it was until Damarius pushed me back and said, "All right, man, I was trying to tell you. He's crazy. Don't give me credit, but I do have your back. I done already got you taken to the office once with the cheating thing, now be sensible. If you think it ain't happen with him and Tori, let it go. Make it seem like it doesn't matter."

Everything Damarius was saying made complete sense. That's exactly what I was thinking earlier. Why did I stand so hot and bothered, acting like a maniac on Marlon?

Coach Robinson came on the field and said, "What's going on here? Boys, get yo behinds up and stretch. Now the whole team gotta do more laps 'cause of y'all foolishness. Now you get to do some suicides and extra laps 'cause of somebody else's mistake, and it's about daggone time that you run some laps for me, anyway. Football is a team sport."

When we got off the field, it was another scene that stopped me dead in my tracks. Tori was standing there oohing and cooing over Marlon. He ran straight up to her and kissed her in front of the whole team. I just walked right past them, couldn't even look at them.

"Oh, so you see it's true, now, huh? She left you for me." Marlon said, trying to rattle me up again.

It worked, but I didn't let him know. His words got to me, but what the heck could I do? Truthfully, I didn't want her. So if she wanted Marlon, why should I care?

"Son, can I talk to you for a minute?" my dad asked when I came into the house.

I was still on shaky ground with him. I didn't wanna answer his question. I felt like just making up some flaky lie 'bout me being busy. But the urgency in his voice seemed like something was going on, so I sat down at the kitchen table with him and uncovered the dish my mom left out for me.

"You didn't wash your hands," my dad said as if I needed his parenting.

"Just came from football practice, Dad. Just took a shower, I'm straight. What's up?" I was aggravated then.

"Son, I don't want what you saw the other day to come between us. Your mom and I are having some serious problems, and what you walked in on wasn't planned. It wasn't ongoing and nothing has happened."

"If that makes you feel better to tell me that, Dad, then cool. Anything else?"

"Come on, Son. Don't play me like that."

"What's wrong, Dad? You think I'm just supposed to forget seeing you with your arms wrapped around another woman? I haven't, and I won't. You told Mama yet?" I asked him boldly.

He sat up in the chair sorta fidgeting.

"I thought you wanted to talk man to man. I can ask you whatever I want, right?" I knew I had him on the fence.

"Seeing that you asked that question, I can tell you that I haven't told your momma yet."

Then I was the one that started fidgeting. I looked down at my food and went over to warm it in the microwave. Why'd he throw this back on me?

"Why haven't you told your mom yet, Son?"

"As you been saying all along, Dad," I said without looking at him, "I need to stay out of grown folks' business. That was a bed you made, I'll let you lie in it. This ain't no Monopoly game. You don't have any 'Get out of jail free' cards. I do expect you to deal with this."

"Come on, now. You know your mom don't need to know this, I don't wanna hurt her."

"Dad, Mom ain't no dummy. She already knows something is up with you," I said as I grabbed my plate out the microwave and sat back down again.

I just wished the conversation was already over. I don't know why I was going down one way and my dad was going down the other and we couldn't seem to walk together. Be on the same page. Be on one cord. And it was frustrating.

"You know your dad's not perfect, and I already told you that nothing got started with her. It's over."

"Naw, I just want you to think about this. You already told me to treat ladies right, like I wanted somebody to treat my sister. I'm making a few mistakes here and there, but for the most part your example ain't making it easier."

"Oh, come on, Son. That ain't fair."

"I'm just saying, Dad. Let's be real with it. The way you treating Mom is how you want Payton's husband to treat her one day? They go through hard times, go through something a lil' tough . . . It's cool if her man steps out, right? That's what you want for your daughter?"

Holding his head down he said, "You know that's not what I want."

"Well, don't set rules for me that you can't even abide by yourself."

"This is a 'do as I say' not 'do as I do' relationship that you and I have." He looked at me like he was the man.

"A deacon of the church," I said as I got up and walked away from the table, showing him I was a man, too.

My dad didn't stop me. Wise move. He knew we both needed space.

Two days later, I came home and found my mom packing. She was crying and screaming while my dad was trying to take stuff away from her and put it back in the drawers. It was pandemonium in there.

"What's going on?" I quickly asked, wishing I didn't have to interfere in their relationship.

"Your dad's having an affair with his secretary, Junior! Did you know that?"

I couldn't believe my mom actually told me that. I just stood there, choking. I didn't know what to do.

My dad tried to block my view. "Pat, don't put that boy into this. Son, go on. Your mom and I are fine."

"No, we're not. We're gonna be separated in a minute. I'm going to a hotel," my mother said as she headed out the door with some clothes hanging out her bulging suitcase.

I took it from her. "Mom, *Mom*. You always told me I can't run away from problems. I ain't saying what he did or didn't do, I'm just saying y'all got something special, so don't go throwing it away and all. You know he loves his family."

"But he doesn't love me anymore!" she said as she fell into my arms.

My dad stood right behind her and touched her shoulder. "I do love you, baby. Maybe we can't be together right now. Maybe you're not the one that needs to leave. Maybe I do."

My mom just cried harder and dropped the suitcase to the

ground. I held on to her tight, looking at my dad with accusing eyes. Eyes that were so angry with him and disappointed in his leadership. Sorta thinking that he wasn't ready to have my mom back in the first place.

However, I knew deep down inside that the last thing I wanted to hear him say was he wanted to move out. Sometimes people are better off not together. I knew that ever since Tori got all crazy on me. We'd grown apart.

"Go cool off, Dad," I said. "Don't nobody need to do nothing hasty right now, neither you nor Mom."

He patted me on the shoulder, squeezed between our embrace, grabbed his keys and headed out. My mom continued crying. I never had to console her like that. Even a couple of weeks ago when I caught her crying she told me that she was fine.

My embrace was what she needed right now to keep her up. I was going nowhere. I wanted my folks to stay together. But if my pops left her, she'd always have me. I had to stay strong.

Weeping she said, "Thank you, baby. I know it's hard for you, Son, to be hearing this tough stuff."

~ 11 ~

Winning the Crown

"**Y**ou guys getting all dressed up for this homecoming dance like it's something major!" I said to my boys as we changed in the locker room after winning another game.

"You know a brotha just like to get clean every now and then," Damarius said as he spun around trying to show off his black pin-striped suit.

Cole came up to me and asked, "You going to the dance, right, Perry? You know I wouldn't want you to be bummed out about people talking about you and Amandi."

"Man, forget about it. That's old." I looked at my blue suit that I had brought just in case.

Damarius muttered, "You didn't wanna get with her, anyway. She probably got something."

I took my towel and popped him with it across the head. "Boy, you one to talk. I'm going to the dance. I'm just mad that I didn't get both of y'all to join the Beautillion. Talkin' about men cleaning up nice . . ."

Damarius took his collar and turned it up all the way. He spun around like he was fly, put on some dark shades, rolled one pants leg up to his knee and left the other one long. He was so crazy.

"You don't think they'll let me in the Beautillion with this getup on, do ya?" he teased.

"Naw, brah, you can't wear the tux like that."

"That's what I'm saying. Here at homecoming, I get to sport my tux just the way I like it."

"I hear ya."

Cole asked, "I look okay for real?"

We both nodded. The big boy was stepping in his fly coat with long tails. He had even put on cologne. For Cole that was a big deal.

I couldn't believe two weeks had gone by since I had had so much turmoil in my life. Seeing Tori with Marlon was definitely a lot to take. Having rumors spread all around the school wasn't cool, either, and having my mom leap into my arms because of heartbreak took a piece of my heart out.

My folks still hadn't worked out all their drama. They didn't think I knew that they now slept in separate bedrooms, but I knew. Although at least with both of them under the same roof, there was some hope.

When I got to the party I stood just observing people, and I was content. I didn't have to dance or be cooped up with a girl. I was actually having a good time seeing everyone enjoy themselves.

Then my eyes skimmed and saw Marlon laughing and huffing in some girl's face. And before my eyes could roam away, I glanced back at him and realized that the girl he was talking to wasn't Tori. What was up with that? Or did I even have to ask? Soon as she let her guard down and got close to that loser, he took advantage of her and went on to conquer more.

Before I could even spend more energy focusing on Tori, Damarius and Cole found me.

"Come on, boy. It's time to get crowned," Cole said as he hit me.

"Man, please," I said, "I don't have this."

Damarius mouthed off, "Yeah, I could have been home-coming king, but I told folks to vote for my boy."

"D, that won't help the way people been talking about me. My name's been mud around here," I said, not caring either way.

"Trust me, dog, you won." Damarius looked real serious.

I wasn't really listening when they announced the ninth-grade and tenth-grade court. However, when they announced the eleventh-grade court, I was ready to hear Tori's name, but I didn't. It was another girl, the same chick that I saw with Marlon earlier. And when he won eleventh-grade prince, the two of them made a passionate statement before the crowd.

Then the announcer declared that Amandi and I won homecoming king and queen. At first I thought it must've been a joke. I didn't even wanna go up on the stage, but I did. I sure wasn't gonna dance with her. She needed no ideas from me that I thought she had it going on.

So when the princesses and princes for the underclass-men got in the middle of the dance floor to dance and they called for the king and queen to join in, I motioned for Damarius to wear my crown and walk Amandi down there. Amandi looked like her plans had been ruined. Then I saw Tori move expeditiously through the crowd. Something was telling me she wasn't all right.

Instinctively, I followed her. Indirectly, I did feel sorta responsible. Trying desperately to get with Marlon was such a down move on her part. How could she possibly care for him?

She turned around and said, "What do you want, Perry? What are you doing following me? Just leave me alone, okay!"

"I'm really concerned about you."

"I finally realized I made a bad choice and now I have to suffer the consequences," she responded in tears.

I wanted to ask her a personal question, like how far did she go with Marlon? But by looking at her devastated face, I didn't need to ask the obvious.

"Look, I'm real sorry about all this."

She sniffed and held back her emotions. "What's done is done. Congratulations on winning homecoming king. I'm really happy for you."

We held hands for a moment, and I hugged her tight. With my embrace I was saying, *"Be strong, girl. Hang tight. Be the Tori I know you can be."* With the look she gave me when we let go, I had the satisfaction of believing she would be okay.

Sunday after church, I was at the monthly Beautillion meeting. As soon as I walked in the place, I wondered how in the world my mother had talked me into doing this. Though I'd teased Damarius and Cole about them not wanting to get refined, I, too, wasn't up for all the polishing. But I needed to get the negative thoughts out my mind quickly, or the next two hours would seem like twenty-four.

This time the fraternity brothers from Omega Psi Phi were giving the presentation. And they knew how to break the ice for all of us. They came in stepping in their gold boots, gold construction hats, purple shirts and olive army-style pants. Decked out, they were looking bad! And on top of that, they were hype.

"All right, all right," they chanted.

After the guys got our attention, they gave us their history and then asked questions about what we just heard. Maybe schools needed to take a page from this method of teaching. Everybody, even Saxon, could answer every question.

The taller, built dude said, "I'm Cleo Armstrong and this is my partner, Sylvester Blue. We are here today to talk to you guys about how you treat a young lady."

"The actual topic," Mr. Blue said, "is being a prince on a date."

Saxon just chuckled. Mr. Armstrong came straight over to him, grabbed him by his shirt and lifted him up. Saxon was quiet then.

"Something funny?" Mr. Armstrong questioned.

I knew if some of the ladies who were in this program would've seen how the Omegas were handling our session, they'd be tripping. However, we boys knew they deserved respect, and they were gon' take it if they didn't get it. We all sat up in our seats. Even tough Saxon apologized.

"Naw, man. I'm just playing with ya. I ain't mad at you, brother," Cleo said as he straightened out Saxon's shirt. "But I'm glad I was able to prove a point. When you're in a leadership role, there's a certain way you should act."

A lot of us looked confused. *Dating? Relationships?* What was this guy talking about?

"How many of you young men believe in God?" All ten of us raised our hands. "How many of you young men think that you're gonna get married one day?"

Saxon left his hand down. Nine of us raised them up. As they started counting, he eventually raised his hand up, too.

"Yeah, I'll probably be like forty-five, but I will marry one day," Saxon joked.

I had no doubts he believed his own bull.

Then Mr. Blue went on to tell us that one day when we got married and believed God's principles for our union, then we as men would be deemed as head of household. He told us we would be looked upon to lead and he didn't think we could learn how to do that overnight. He said that we needed to be taught how to treat women right, even in our dating relationships.

Mr. Armstrong said, "If we would one day love and respect

our wives, then in dating relationships, we ought to be able to be sincere and care about the young women we take out."

A lot of us coughed on that one. Not me. I understood where they were coming from. One day I did want a family. One day I did want to have some woman follow me. And as I thought about how my dad had been leading lately, I knew deep down I didn't want that, even though my actions weren't that different from my father's. We both were committed to someone else and got busted.

Cleo Armstrong said, "See, all that being a dog, trying to be a player and have many women and stuff is for punks. True men of valor, men with principles and integrity, can date a few honeys at a time, but keep everything on the up and up honestly. Not trying to take anybody for anything. Having serious relationships right now is kinda crazy, anyway. You guys are only seniors in high school. You're 'bout to enter into college. Trust me there are going to be plenty of fine babes to blow your mind. What you don't want to do now is break somebody's heart. That stuff comes back on ya. And I believe in karma."

I thought about what he was saying and I certainly knew I needed to get on my knees and ask for forgiveness 'cause I didn't want anything negative to come back on me. Or had it already? Amandi had ran her mouth about me still being a virgin. Her loud mouth was ruining my reputation. And had I done so much damage to Tori that I hadn't even received my payback yet? If that was the case, I did need to start praying.

I blurted out, "So do y'all think if you dog out a girl, that stuff will come back on you?"

"More or less. I mean, we've lived long enough to know that when you do wrong, you pay for it in some form," Sylvester Blue answered.

We went on and on to talk about how you should end one relationship before stepping into another one.

Cleo said, "And even though some girls can never take no for an answer at least when you say it's over verbally, you're not responsible for what they do after you move on. It's when you make them think you down with them and you still having fun in other places that it's your fault. That's when character gets into question."

We ended up doing some role reversals. In one scene, a guy broke up with a girl. In one version, she took it well; in one version she didn't take it so well. We all came away learning to take the high road. Being the gentleman, bowing out and not forcing yourself on her was the right way to go.

We also talked about other dating do's for gentlemen, like holding the door for our date. Or when a guy asks a girl out, he should pay and try and always meet her parents before taking her out. From what the Omegas say, we can definitely earn brownie points with the ladies this way.

Though my parents had told me this growing up, I enjoyed the session given by two cool guys. I got the message. I knew I needed to tighten up a little bit. Even though I could dog out some women because of my popularity status, it didn't mean I should. I didn't really want Tori anymore. My feelings for her had changed, and I was glad things were over. And Amandi really wasn't my speed. So I'm glad we were over as well.

Whenever I got that next girl God would send my way, I was gonna remember all the things I'd learned here. And hopefully implement them to make God proud. I was a gentleman and I now knew I needed to treat women better.

"Oh, now since you homecoming king and all you don't have time to do no favors for your big sister, huh?"

"Now why you had to throw that all in my face?" I asked Payton over the phone as she was trying to bully me into coming to some Fellowship of Christian Athletes high school retreat.

I was not excited about going to the woods with some people I didn't even know. Supposedly, it was this cool resort site in Stone Mountain, Georgia. Driving two and a half hours to be way up on a mountain really wasn't my idea of fun.

"Perry, consider the invitation. There's gonna be tons of athletes there."

"Sis, I just don't wanna drive there."

"Okay. I'll call you right back."

I just knew I had her off my back. But then, ten minutes later the phone rang and it was Payton again.

"I talked to Tad and he told me his cousin Savoy is coming with one of her girlfriends. He talked to her, and she said that since you're only ten minutes away, as long as her dad says it is cool for her to pick you up, then she would drive. You have any more excuses?"

I knew this was a Christian event, and I felt sorta bad. However, I had to admit that after learning Savoy was going, my interests were a little bit higher. I kept my thoughts in check, though. After all, we were just friends and all, and I knew she had a boyfriend. However, she did come to my birthday party, so I knew she had some interest in me, even if it was only a little bit.

"So when are we going to know if her dad says it's okay?" I asked my sister.

"See, I knew you'd be down to come to this thing if it was all about girls and football. Boy, you better get your life straight. Lately, you've been real excited about the wrong stuff. You need to be excited about God like that."

"Pay, don't be preaching to me. Be happy I'll come."

"Tad's gon' talk to his uncle. Call you later." My sister got off the phone with much attitude.

After I hung up, I felt compelled to get on my knees and pray. It'd been a long time since I actually gave God his real reverence. My sister thought I didn't hear stuff she said. Actually, a lot of times I didn't pay her much mind. But a lot of times the things she mouthed off to me made sense to me.

So I prayed:

"Lord, I have been really caught up with football lately. And you know girls have been on my priority list, too. I'm just keeping it real. I'm willing to go on this retreat this weekend and maybe it's all for the wrong reasons. But if it actually works out and I go, help me understand You more. I'll be open-minded. Amen."

Three days later, I was in the car with Savoy and her friend Ellis headed to the Atlanta area for the FCA retreat. Ellis was a pretty girl: dark mocha-colored skin, petite, with a short, fly curly hairdo, curves in the right places and spunky. She was checking me out from the moment I got in the car.

Savoy, on the other hand, was sorta hard to read. She was cordial and nice and everything, but because she was concentrating on the road, it was hard to make her out. I wasn't trying to win her over or anything, but I didn't want the ride to be a drag. Remembering my seminar on how to take the lead, even though this wasn't a dating relationship, I was a perfect gentleman.

So I tried to ease the tension and said, "Savoy, thanks for letting me tag along with you guys. I'll be able to drive if you want. Pops said our insurance would cover it if something was to happen."

"No problem, Mr. Skky. I appreciate you saying that. I'll keep that in mind."

"Ooh, ooh!" her friend teased. "Girl, he's a keeper."

Savoy made a smirk.

"I ain't talking 'bout for you, you got already got a man. I'm the single one. We're already bonded. His name's Perry, my name's Ellis."

I was confused. I didn't know what that had to do with anything. And then all of a sudden this girl said, "We're a clothing line. We already go together. Get it? Perry Ellis . . ."

The three of us just started laughing. Then Savoy put on this gospel CD by J Moss. As I leaned my head back and listened to the some of the words, I was just taken over by something I hadn't felt in a while. It wasn't about the ride. It wasn't about the girls. It wasn't about football. It was about worshipping God.

I just remembered the chorus singing out so well, "No matter who or what we are, we must pray." It was like before I had even got to the retreat, God was answering my prayer. He was letting me know Him more.

And this song was saying that to get to know God more, I just needed to give praise and give thanks to Him. I learned to just be into Him and expect good things in return. The three of us spent the next hour talking about just that. Ellis tried to get off subject every now and then, but Savoy and I knew we were very focused where God was concerned.

Stone Mountain Park was absolutely beautiful. They had some events on the campground. But most of the stuff was taking place in the Evergreen Hotel. It was a Marriott resort. My sister had hooked me up. Although I was used to being in nice hotels because of all the recruiting, this was better. It was just nice to get away and not have to worry about someone wanting something.

At first I was excited because I thought I was going to get to know Savoy better. Before the end of the first day, however, I was beginning to know God more. It was an experience I couldn't explain.

The Georgia Tech chaplain I'd met a couple of weeks ago was giving the evening message. Hearing him present the Gospel charged me to want to live my life for God. He was absolutely dynamic and passionate. He talked about athletics, but then he took stories from the Bible and made them apply to how he walked with God.

So I sat on my seat and listened while he closed his sermon. "So, athletes, if you're in that crunch time and need something positive to happen in your life, remember Moses' story. God can deliver. Remember when you're thrown into the lions' den, God can get you out. When you sense the Holy Spirit leading you to do something that you and everyone else thinks is crazy, just follow that intuition. Keep letting God lead you. Remember Noah's flood was going to come, and yours will, too. You need to be prepared. And under God's umbrella, He protects you and keeps you safe. In order to follow God and know that He delivers, you gotta trust Him. And so I close with the story of Peter. God said he could walk on water, but he just had to get out of the boat first. So wherever you are in your life, get out of the boat. Know that God's got it. Know that Jesus wants to praise you and intervene. Even if you have accepted God into your life, make nothing more important than Him."

I sat there with tears in my eyes because I had been more focused on many other things—grades, girls, cars, football, scholarships, money—everything but God. I felt bad, I felt sorry. Savoy took my hand, and I didn't even notice until I looked up and saw her eyes were just as red and welled up as mine. Together we walked toward the front of the aisle while the soft music was playing.

We recommitted ourselves to Christ as the chaplain closed by saying, "Most people are either brought out of a situation, in a situation or about to get into one. As athletes, you're faced with all three, all the time. But to be victorious whether you win a game, lose a game, get hurt, stay healthy, have to deal with the fame, have to deal with standing on the sidelines, or whatever it is, be a part of God's team, and you'll be victorious. It's not about winning the trophy, being MVP or state champs . . ."

He paused for a second and let all heads be bowed. I knew what he was saying. I understood it. I felt it as I squeezed Savoy's hand tighter. I hoped she got it.

The chaplain said, "It's about winning the crown."

~ 12 ~

Praising His Name

It'd been a week since the retreat. As soon as I got back from my mountaintop experience I went to the mall and bought my own J Moss CD. Not only did I understand every song, I felt myself connecting more and more with God through the music.

My mom even knew his songs from me playing them over and over in my room. When she passed by to get to the laundry room, she sometimes heard it 'cause my room was right next to there. She even heard the music outside when I blasted it while I was cutting the grass or washing the cars.

Since my dad was scarcely around the place, she and I had a much stronger bond. We both wanted to focus more on Christ. We were all about lifting Him up. And it wasn't about God coming through. He'd already done enough by sending His Son to die on a cross for our sins. It was about us just giving God glory. Letting Him be enough to fill us, though life was somewhat uncertain. I needed God to show me what college to go to.

As she started preparing Thanksgiving dinner, I went into the kitchen with my iPod in hand and started the music all over. When she turned around, I saw that her eyes were watery. I didn't know if it was from the onions she was chopping for the stuffing or if she was sad. Either way, as soon as I played an up-tempo beat on the CD, she smiled.

"Thank you, baby. That's what I needed to hear."

I went and wrapped my arms around her neck. "Mom, what's up? You can talk to me. I know I'm your son, and it might be a little weird to unload on me, but I'm stronger than you think. How am I supposed to grow up and be a man if you don't let me help you?"

She placed her right hand on my cheek and rubbed it gently. Then she looked into my eyes and said, "You are a young man, aren't you, Perry?"

She had called me Junior for so long it felt kinda weird hearing her call me Perry. I think it caught me off guard. She just stared at me.

"You look so much like your daddy. Ain't that funny! I met him when I was a freshman in college. Then he was around your age."

"So that's what you're doing, Mom? Thinking 'bout him?" I asked harshly, as I took her hand off my cheek and held it firmly.

She looked away. "Son, I don't wanna worry you with that."

Mom started back preparing the Thanksgiving meal. By then, my stomach was growling. This wasn't about me being filled with food. This was about me being filled with comfort that my mom was going to be okay with my dad maybe gone and me leaving soon.

She sensed that I had something heavy on my mind. She turned around and said, "I haven't seen your father in a while, you know that? Even in separate bedrooms, he'd get up early in the morning and come in late at night. I don't know what he is doing in his life and I don't know what's going to happen with that man. I don't know if I really want him anymore. But let's not think about that now. Your sister's on her way home, and she is stopping to pick up your grandmother."

We hadn't seen my dad's mom in a while. I hated that because I knew she'd been through it since she lost her husband. My granddad died of natural causes the Christmas before. I just hoped our time together would be civil. Payton and my grandma didn't know that there was stuff between my folks. I hoped I didn't mess up the evening and let it out.

My mom shared my same concerns. "I'm not looking forward to dinner, Son. Payton loves your dad to death, and your grandmother loves her son to death. And right about now he's one of my least favorite people. I don't want my feelings to show. This is going to be stressful for us."

"Ma, you know I got your back."

"I know that, baby. But it shouldn't be about that on Thanksgiving. It's not about being sad, it's about being thankful for what God has given you. And that's what I'm going to try to do: appreciate you being concerned and reading through my distress. But I'm not gon' break. God's making me whole. He's doing amazing work for you, too. I've been seeing you skipping around to His beat. We gotta keep being into Him and not our own problems. It's going to be a great day. Okay, baby?"

"Yes, ma'am," I said. Then I asked another question. "When can we dig into the turkey?"

"It'll be about four hours, boy. Here," she said as she sliced me a piece of ham. "Go relax."

At dinner it was sorta like my mom had said earlier. Dinner was weird with the five of us. My mom was quiet. My grandma and sister were acting like my dad was royalty or something. I couldn't even look my dad's way.

My grandmother started raving about how much she loved the new car my dad had bought her. "Ooh, chile, I'm getting so many compliments. Can't even leave the church parking lot without people crowding around to see my car. Your father started that car dealership so long ago, I'm sure we didn't think it was going to turn into what you've made it, Son."

Man, it was just a car. Dad didn't do anything great, he'd just given her one right off the dealership lot. It wasn't no money coming directly out his pockets. Grandma needed to be thanking God for having good health and a right mind for seventy-five years. But of course I was respectful, and didn't reveal my thoughts and kept eating the great food.

My sister was so excited about the brand-new, four-bedroom condo my dad had just purchased for her. She'd be able to collect money from a couple of her friends who were going to be her housemates, and enjoy the extra money he'd allow her to keep.

"My place is so nice, y'all. Daddy, thank you again for buying it!"

She didn't even thank my mom. My dad's money was her money, too. I knew my moms felt a little bad. I could tell when she looked away and dropped her head.

When dinner was over, my mom and my grandmother cleaned up. My dad came to my room and said, "Son, you wanna watch some football with me?"

"I'm straight," I said, hoping he would get the point and leave. We weren't cool like that no more.

"Hey, I know you still might be mad at me, but you can't stay mad at me forever. You need your father," he said.

"Oh, I've got my Father. One who's there for me all the time and never messes up. And at this time, that's good for me. You don't need me on your side, anyway. You got your cheerleading session going on: your mom and Payton giving you all the praises."

He looked at me with nothing to say. I mean, what could

he say? It was what it was. He walked out, closed my door and let me be.

A few minutes later, Payton came in, going on and on about how my mom was being so cold to my dad. I had no problem with getting her straight on the spot.

"Look, he ain't been here. I know dad's perfect in your eyes, but I caught him with his secretary, for your information. So next time you wanna come down on somebody, make sure you have all the facts before you judge. At the end of the day, Sis, you gave all the honor to the wrong parent."

Her jaw dropped. I walked out the room, leaving her with what I just said. Our family was a mess, and her getting in the middle of it wasn't making it any better.

Two days later I saw my sister again. She was cheering at the Georgia vs. Georgia Tech football game at Georgia. And I was so proud of her. She was the only brown speck out there doing her thing. Their stadium was beautiful, with 92,000 fans in red screaming, "Dogs! Dogs! Dogs!"

It was my last recruiting trip of the year. And my parents came, since this was Payton's school. People didn't know the real deal; everyone thought that everything was good with the Skky family. I just prayed that God would actually make everything good with my family so I wouldn't have to worry about my parents fighting and embarrassing me in front of the world.

Lance Shadrach was there, too. It was interesting hearing the coaches go on and on about what a dynamite player he was. The last few games of the season, he'd turned it out. He was trying to take my place as our state's number-one recruit.

He came over to me and said, "Hey, Perry, what's up, dude?"

"I'm straight, man. I hear you been ballin'."

Lance laughed. We chatted for a sec. Then the recruiting coordinator ushered him away.

I spotted Saxon. He was talking to a coach. The wide receiver coach was all up on Saxon. Truth be told, I was having a problem with them getting all excited about other guys.

I wasn't no scrub player. Shoot, I was high-placed, too. *What was that about?* I wondered.

Shortly after, Saxon came over and said, "Seems like I'm the guy everybody wanna get with, huh? Boy, you better post up some more numbers. You trying to be humble and share that ball too much."

"Boy, you crazy. Like I care or need your advice."

Saxon replied, "Oh, you care all right. Georgia has only one slot for a wide receiver, and it looks like it's gon' be me. The other school for your state is getting beat bad today, maybe they still want you."

I was so angry. I tried not to let it show in front of Saxon, but I could tell he was getting the message. He knew the big buttons to push, and I let him push them hard. I was fueled up.

After the game I walked down the sidelines to see the scoreboard showing Georgia Tech got beat by Georgia by twenty-one points; I looked at the Georgia Tech chaplain. Thankfully, the Lord brought my attention back to Him.

"Skky," he said, as he came over and shook my hand.

"I didn't get a chance to talk to you last week, but I heard your sermon at the FCA retreat."

"Oh, you were on the mountain?"

"Yes, sir. My sister's a cheerleader at Georgia."

"Oh, you talking about Tad Taylor's girlfriend? Yeah, okay. I forgot her name."

"It's Payton," I said.

"Yeah, Payton. Sweet girl."

"You did a great job planning that event. I just wanted to say that your talk moved me and made think about how I need to put God first in my life."

"I know we've been trying to recruit you to Tech. Any chance we can get you there? They'd give you all the respect you could want. Certainly we can continue to get more into the Word."

"I really haven't decided yet," I said.

"I know, I know. I'm just messing with you," the chaplain said. "But you look like you lost your best friend."

"It's just the recruiting thing. It's tough. I don't know what's the right decision with the places that I want to go. It seems like they're sorta losing interest in me 'cause I didn't sign up in time."

"No need to rush it. No need to be upset if it seems like schools are choosing other guys. They choose them according to their needs. And sometimes they pick the guys and have to move you to a different position. You want to make sure the right school chooses you for the skills that you have. Don't keep comparing yourself to other people. You're doing the best you can. Keep believing in God. You say you heard my sermon: cling to it. Keep your focus on Him."

My parents, Payton and I had dinner out and then we headed home. On the drive back, Payton still wasn't acting nice toward our mother. I did feel stronger, but God was going to have to lead me to the right place. With the silence in the car I leaned my head back, placing my family and future in the hands of God. With the peace, I fell asleep.

The next day Damarius made me promise I'd come over his house to meet some of his relatives. The three-bedroom, two-bathroom ranch could hold about twenty people comfortably. I was amazed to see about one hundred folks there

in the backyard and front, plus people eating in the bedrooms and people sitting on the floor everywhere. It was
smelling good in there.

I hit him up on the cell phone to let him know I was in the
house. Then all of a sudden, I heard a scream.

It was Damarius. "Hey, y'all! My boy's here! The star is
here. Y'all back on out the way and let Perry through."

He was on his cell. When his family moved to let me
through the family room, we found each other and gave a
friendly hug. I was hungry, but I had to stay beside Damarius
for another forty minutes to meet and greet. Everybody in-
terrupted their meal to shake my hand.

"Come on, D. I ain't got to meet everybody, do I?" I whispered to him.

"Aww, y'all, he's modest."

His dad came up to me and said, "Well, since my son ain't
going pro, I have to treat Perry good. He's small now, but
wait til he signs for the big money."

Damarius's granddad slowly came over to me. He was so
frail and limping with a cane. He then looked me in the eye
and said, "Uh-huh. I see he got potential. The top in the
state."

He listed all my stats. Told me what games he was most
impressed with and what I need to improve on as I took my
behind to college. Damarius even took one of the footballs
from his room, and I signed it and gave it to his granddad.

"Boy, I know you're hungry," his father said as he came
over to me again.

"No, I'm fine. I'm fine," I said, although really I was dying
to get a taste of that barbecue chicken and ribs.

I couldn't even eat without someone staring at my food. I
just smiled back at people and tried not to let them know
that their stares were really bothering me. Then I heard conversations all around me.

"Probably come outta college early. He could make a million dollars," I heard a man say.

"A million? Please! He'll probably have a signing bonus for about twenty mil," someone responded.

And then some ladies on the other side said, "I know his mama has to be so proud. She's got a football star for a son."

"Yeah. But it's not like they need any more money."

"I guess the rich keeps on getting richer, huh?"

"We all packed all over him like a colony fighting over a piece of chicken."

"He is a cute little boy, though," a lady said.

"You need to hook him up with Clarice."

"Say what? Chile, *please.*"

At that moment I choked on a piece of chicken, trying to contain my laugh. I didn't wanna eat and run, but I was sorta tired of being put on display. I quickly played a couple of games with Damarius and his cousins. The last game wore me out.

"Aww, man, you ain't 'bout to jet now, are you?" Damarius asked.

"Yeah. I gotta get on home."

"What's wrong with you, Perry? You seem . . . I don't know."

"No, I'm cool. It's just that—"

"What, my people treating you too special? I know you used to it by now. You on the news every Friday night and you done been to the best schools in the ACC and the SEC for recruiting trips. Get used to the spotlight."

"Boy, you crazy. I ain't nobody. I'm just a plain person. But it's hard to explain."

"You'll get over that way of thinking," he said as he patted me on the back.

I got in the car and played my Christian CD. I didn't wanna get the big head. I wanted to stay humble.

The next day I had to go to dinner at Justin's house. It was a sit-down Sunday feast. I was meeting his people, but it was the same overkill. *"Perry is the best at this. Perry can do that."* Like I was some TV star or something.

After dinner I wasn't at all frustrated when his little cousin who was in the 4th grade asked me to come outside and throw balls. He said he wanted to be a quarterback one day so I told him to try it out on me.

"You got skills, lil' man," I said.

"You know it!" he yelled out.

He hailed another one my way. I could tell he had been working on this.

Before we went inside, he said, "Perry, can I ask you a question?"

"Sure."

"I play middle school ball and I'm really nervous that I'm not gonna be as good as you when I get to high school. You got any advice for me? I want people to think I'm the man, too, when I get up there."

"That's not why I'm standing here in front of you now with a little respect." He had a puzzled look on his face. "What I'm trying to say is I play football because I love it, not because I want people to cheer my name. Being able to go off to school on a scholarship to play college ball is a dream of mine. So is making it into the NFL. If I don't play hard now, then I won't be as good in the big leagues. I can tell you this: I believe and trust in God. Do you believe in God?" He nodded his head. "Well, keep praying for Him to help you. And remember: do everything you can to glorify God. It's not about football or people screaming your name, but in the end you use your playing football to get people more lifted in Him."

He smiled. "Oh, I got it!"

"So, I'm not saying don't work for what you want. Keep on practicing, keep on hoping, keep on believing and keep on praying. Either way you gon' be all right." As I talked to the little guy I was talking to myself as well. "Just remember, it's not about people thinking you're all that. Just stay focused and keep praising His name."

~ 13 ~

Taking Deep Risks

"All right, men, this is the beginning of the moment you guys have been waiting for all season long," Coach Robinson said to us before our first playoff performance. "You're superior to this team in every way. But don't be fooled. Don't think that you're all that. They still can find a way to beat you. They're probably gonna come out here with the best plays you've ever seen just so they can defeat the highest seed. We have three games left at home to play and if we win, then we're headed on to the Dome. I want each of you to take a few minutes to reflect before we go out there and warm up. Don't take this game lightly. The best team today wins."

As we gathered around Coach Robinson, we were hyped. We were excited. We were ready for battle. I had come close to getting to the Dome on other teams, but I never actually got there. We also never had home field advantage. Since this year had gone so quickly, this was the time to make a difference.

I just looked around and watched some of the guys get taped up extra tight. Other guys were hitting each other with pads, making sure they were prepared for the battle to come. Some of the players were studying playbooks.

And then I noticed Damarius in the corner. He was real jittery. His cleats were shaking. He was wrapping his wrists real tight. He was bopping his head up and down. I didn't know what was wrong with my friend.

"Hey, dude. What's going on wit you?" I asked as I hit his shoulder pads.

"I don't know, Perry, man. I'm just nervous 'bout this one. Our old coach is here. And he told me on the phone earlier this week that he was coming to see me."

"What? He's coming to scout you for Fort Valley?"

Damarius chewed on his fingers and said, "Yeah, he said that if I pull up a few grades, then he might finally take me for a ride."

"Well, you know what you gotta do. You gotta get out there and do your thing, man."

My friend kept his head down. The boy I knew as a show-boater seemed deflated before he could even get started to show off. I felt compelled to pull him out of his slump.

"I don't understand this, Damarius. You been wanting this all year. You've just wanted a chance for a shot at college ball. This is your day for another big interception. It was your play that got us to the playoffs. Our defense is tight. You own the secondary," I said, hoping he'd feel me and agree.

"Wish I had something to take the pressure away," he muttered. "Just something to take my mind off this and take my brain up another level."

"Boy, what you talking 'bout?" I asked angrily. "You talking about drugs? Steroids or something?"

"Everybody ain't got natural skills, all right?"

"Be for real. You don't need to throw your future away with nothing like that."

"Yeah, right. You know if you was to get hurt one day, you'd be wanting to take something to pump your game up a notch, too."

"First of all, D, you ain't hurt. And second, you don't

know me if you think I'd do some dumb crap like that. Look here, I ain't trying to force the Word of God on you or nothing, but since you talking about what I would do, I'm trying to pray more. You believe in God, don't you, man?"

"Yeah, I know the Man Upstairs."

"Well, talk to Him," I said as I placed my hand on his shoulder. "Let him know that you need His help down here."

I walked away, leaving my friend in his deep thoughts. I knew I was gonna pray for him but I wanted him to take his words to God himself. This was a big game—even though Lucy Laney was favored to win by twenty-one points. Like Coach said, "You don't take anything for granted."

Since the guys in the locker room also looked timid, I went to talk to Coach Robinson and asked, "Hey, Coach, you mind if I lead the team prayer when we take the field?"

"Perry, that's fantastic," Coach Robinson said excitedly. "I didn't know you would take that kind of initiative."

Then I actually started second-guessing my decision. I didn't want the guys thinking I was a punk because I started to pray. But I dismissed that thought altogether. Though it wasn't my norm, I knew deep down that anything for God was worth it.

After Coach gave his pep talk, he turned it over to me. I prayed.

"Lord, the pressure is gaining here. Football is our life, and being successful at it is our dream. We're coming to You right now, happy that You allowed us to be healthy and play this game today. Let our minds be clear, and Your will be done. In Jesus's name, Amen."

"You didn't pray for us to win!" Marlon shouted rudely.

I didn't even answer him 'cause I knew my prayer spoke for itself. To me it wasn't about winning and losing. It was about God protecting all my teammates from damnation. I wanted them to find God just as I had. I just wanted us to have peace, and peace that only came from Him.

At halftime when were leading 27-0, the guys came to me and said, "Good prayer, man. Good prayer."

Even Damarius was talking about God being with him. Most of the guys were asking me about my relationship with Him. I didn't know what to share, but I spoke from the heart.

We won the game, but more importantly, guys were being drawn to Christ. My risk of showing how I felt about the Almighty was paying off. To God be the glory.

Two weeks later we had completed our third victory. We were now getting ready for the state championship game. We were slated to play Salem High School in Conyers, Georgia, Lance's school. I'd been hoping his team would get knocked off earlier so we wouldn't have to play them, but I was ready to give it my all. I was going to be a leader during practice.

When Coach gave us a break, I saw Damarius huddled over, like he was about to die. I hurried over to him. Then he started scratching around the seat of his shorts. He was moving his leg from side to side, just squirming. I extended my arms and shrugged my shoulders, giving him that look of bewilderment.

Then he leaned over and said, "Man, you gotta take me to that doctor again. I ain't straight."

"What? D, man, what's up?"

"I don't know, Perry. It ain't no burn or anything."

"Man, you been using protection? I know this lil' problem you got ain't come from Ciara."

"No, no. She been trying to play hard to get, so I just been having fun in other places. I'm just keeping it real. Don't be looking at me like that."

"You done got another disease. What you gon' do about that?" I asked him.

"You think it's a disease?"

"You ain't acting normal! I don't know that much about STDs, but scratching and squirming . . . I don't know."

"Can you take me?"

"We gotta finish practice first, so you gotta wait."

"I don't really need practice today." He gripped between his shorts and fell to his knees. "It's like a sore or something. I don't really feel good."

He didn't want me to put his business out there so I asked Coach to just sit him on the sidelines and then we got special permission to leave early.

When we were on the way to the doctor's office, he was acting like I couldn't get there fast enough.

"I can't explain it. The sensations for the last couple of days haven't been too good. I don't know if I done scratched up my flesh or what's going on."

"I can't believe you got me taking you to the doctor again. Tell me, D, was the sex worth it?"

"It was then, but it sure ain't right now. And I don't know which one of them nasty girls I'm gonna have to go off on. They done gave me something where I have to take medicine again."

I didn't wanna say it to him, but he had better hope it was curable.

After his tests, Dr. Hanceby motioned for Damarius to come into his office.

"Come on, man. Come with me," Damarius said to me.

"Man, those are your test results. I don't wanna go in there," I said emphatically, knowing I didn't want to know his business.

"Doc, is it okay if he comes, you know, like last time?"

Dr. Hanceby replied, "Yes, if it's okay for me to share the results with the both of you."

"Yeah. It's straight. That's my boy. What's going on with me?"

"You have herpes," Dr. Hanceby said with a serious expression to Damarius.

I didn't exactly know what herpes was, but I knew it wasn't something he wanted to have. The doctor wasn't looking optimistic. Damarius wasn't getting the picture.

"So what I got to take, Doc? What I gotta do to get rid of this? My mama got a medical card. I could do the copay. It hurts, seems like it's getting bigger. The back of my leg feels numb. I just need something."

"Well, young man, I've got good news and bad news for you. Which do you want first?"

"Just give it to me straight, Doc. What's up?" Damarius asked.

"The good news is I can give you some medicine to take care of what's ailing you now."

"Well, it ain't no bad news," Damarius said while standing up and hitting himself on the chest, like he was proud of himself.

"Herpes isn't something that has a cure at this time."

All of a sudden, my friend started frowning. Finally he took the doctor seriously and just remained still.

"Well, I thought you just said that you could give me medicine to get rid of this."

"That's medicine for the outbreak and for the symptoms. It will go away temporarily, but for now you'll have this for life."

"I'll always have these outbreaks?" Damarius asked in a deflated tone.

The doctor slowly nodded. It wasn't something that could kill my boy, but it was a lifetime disease. Regardless of what he thought about his few nights of passion with different girls before, clearly, he should have wished he could take all that back.

"So, D, you gon' tell Ciara this, right?" I asked as we drove home.

"Heck naw, man, and you ain't, either," he said forcibly.

I couldn't believe what I was hearing. How selfish! Damarius went on to say that he'd work it out, and that he didn't care about my thoughts on the subject.

When we got to his house, he said, "Man, thanks for the ride, but stay out my business. Everybody ain't no goody-goody like you."

"D, don't feed me that bull. I think you're a punk if you don't tell Ciara what she has been exposed to," I said.

"What, so you gon' front on me like that? Shoot, Perry, stay out my business and my life. You ain't nobody's daddy!"

He got out my car and slammed the door. We were through. I didn't care.

Though it was windy, I was out in my backyard shooting hoops. With the championship game right around the corner, I had too many thoughts running through my mind. I was still out when the sun went down, looking up at the Georgia sky. I took the chance to feel closer to God.

As I turned my face toward the sky when I made a sweet three-point shot, my nose brushed against the wind. To me that felt like God saying, "Boy, I got you! Keep following my path, and you'll be straight."

"Lord, just help me keep it real for You," I prayed. *"Help me be a Christ-like example . . ."*

Before I could finish praying, I heard a car pull up in my driveway all fast. Quickly, I looked up and moved out the way. Cole came rushing over to me.

"I know something's wrong. What you done did, man?" I asked jokingly.

"Man, I messed up everything." Cole was a bundle of nerves.

"What you talking about?" I asked, as I tried to make sense of what he was not saying.

He just paced back and forth. He was mumbling to himself, with his hands pointed toward the sky. He was making circles. He was making me nervous!

"Cole, stop. Tell me what's up."

"It's Briana."

"What about her, she hurt or something?"

"She might be pregnant." He fell to the ground.

I just took the ball and threw it against the backboard. "Man, you serious?"

Brianna was in the eleventh grade, and Cole had just agreed to accept a full scholarship to the University of South Carolina. The two of them didn't need to be nobody's parents. This was a hot mess. Then I realized he said that she *might be* pregnant.

I asked, "So this isn't confirmed?"

"No, no we're not sure. I remember when she told me she didn't want to. But dang, she was looking all good. I nibbled on that ear, it was on! You know I love me some Briana. I couldn't resist! The temptation was there, man. I think she might be pregnant. Her period was supposed to be here last week, and it ain't here yet. What am I gon' do, Perry?"

Why'd he have to ask me for advice? I wasn't trying to get in none of this. I'd lost a friendship giving Damarius advice in his situation and I wasn't gon' get caught up in somebody else's drama and lose another pal. No way!

"You gotta handle this," I told him.

"Perry, I just need you to come over to her house with me, man. She said Tori is over there helping her take tests or whatever. I just need you to come over there with me. Please, Perry? You don't know how this feels."

I was so relieved about that. With Damarius's consequences, it made me happy that I was still abstinent. And Cole had tipped in another reason why my way was the better way.

"I can't drive my car, either. Can you drive my car?"

"All right, man, give me the keys."

I didn't wanna fuss at him as we drove to his girl's crib. He was already feeling miserable enough, but why did my boys have to be so stupid? I hoped this was a false alarm. I hope he'd learned something.

When we got over Briana's house, we didn't have to ask any questions. Tori was sitting there holding Cole's girl. Both of them were crying. I just looked over at Cole, put my hand on his shoulder and gripped it tight. He needed to keep it together and hold up. He was going to be a daddy. He had to step up and be the best one he knew how.

"What we gon' do?" Briana asked as she rushed into his arms. "I can't be a mom!"

Cole just had this dumb look on his face.

"Why did you do this to me, Cole?"

Then she pounded on his chest. I looked at Tori and could only thank God that I hadn't gotten her into this same trouble. Briana just went crazy. Tori tried to calm her down. Cole tried to calm her down. She was just hysterical. She was sad. She didn't want to be a teen mom.

Cole finally spoke up and said, "I'ma take care of this, Briana. You gon' be okay. We gon' get rid of the baby."

As if I wasn't feeling bad enough, those words took me to another level. Did my buddy just say that he was going to take a baby's life before it had a chance to live? *How selfish,* I thought. I rushed over to the two of them and said, "No, no, Cole. There are other options. Adoption or something. Y'all can't kill this baby. That ain't God's will."

"You need to stay up out my business."

"You brought me over here. I can't let y'all do that."

"Yeah, right, Perry. You of all people should understand that I can't pass up no scholarships and stuff. I don't want my life to be over 'cause of no baby."

Tori came over and said, "Yeah, Perry, we gotta let them handle this. I don't agree with that, either, and I wouldn't do it if it was me. That's why I'm not having sex."

Briana just buried her head into Cole's chest.

"I'm ready to get home," I blurted out.

Tori looked up at me and said, "I can take you."

It'd been a while since I talked to her. This wasn't any time to start from where we left off. All I asked God for was peace. And I was getting a little bothered that He couldn't grant me that. I was trying to show my boys how to walk with God, and it bugged me that they wouldn't listen.

Quite frankly, I was tired of being the good boy. Tired of helping everybody out. Tired of putting myself out there when it wasn't benefiting me. I was tired of taking deep risks.

~ 14 ~

Hoping for Relief

"Son, can I talk to you before you get ready to go?" my dad asked seriously as he stood in front of my door.

I really missed him. Not only had he been around the house a lot less, but when he was home, he and I were in different parts of it.

I didn't know what he'd been planning to come in my room and say, but I knew I had to give him the benefit of the doubt and not jump all over him. Though I still I had trouble with some of the things he did, he was my dad and deep down I loved him just as much as I always had. I didn't need to get myself worked up. At least not right before I was about to play the biggest game of my senior year.

I was to play at the Dome in about six hours. I wanted and needed to stay focused. He came in and sat down on the end of my bed. I hadn't remembered him doing that since I was little.

"You know, Perry, I owe you a big apology. This has been a tough year for you. Adding family pressure is more than you needed to handle right now. I've been thinking these last few weeks, and I'm sorry about what you walked in on. Man, I don't have any excuses. It was just sin. I'm trying to deal with that. Not only have I not been a good husband, I haven't been a great father to you, either. I got to choose my own college, you know. My dad basically stepped back and told me that it was time for me to become a big man and make some big decisions. Even though he didn't agree with my choice, he supported it. And he was paying."

We both shared our first laugh in a while together. It felt good. Just that small moment took so much pressure off us.

"Son, I just came to tell you to choose the school that you wanna go to. I still plan on giving my input, but I will let you make your own decision. I'm glad it don't have to come out my pockets, either. You're earning a scholarship. You really should be able to decide."

He held out his arms. I just looked at him for a second. Then his eyes got watery. I had never in my life seen my dad cry. Not even at his own father's funeral. I slid over by him and laid my head on his shoulder and gave him a hug. He gave me three pats on the back. It was a hug like I'd never experienced. And it felt meaningful.

"Go get 'em out there today, partner. You the man," he said to me as we parted.

I'd been to the Dome a couple of times for football games, concerts and conferences. But I'd never gotten the chance to be on the field warming up. Being at the Dome where the Falcons played was a high point in my life, and I didn't know how to contain the feeling.

The whole first quarter I was triple-teamed. When I slid to the right defensive backs were on me. Lance's Seminoles put up 14 points. We had nothing going into halftime. Second half, we got the ball first. They faked it to the running back, and I ran it with full speed. Our leader outran the corner and tipped in on the fake. I caught the ball, and it was over. We had 7. We had a ball game. We had hope. It was a defensive battle in the mix.

Twelve minutes left in the fourth quarter and the score was still 14 to 7.

Coach asked me, "Are you ready for the big play? Can you take this home? Can you at least tie this game, boy?"

Coach gave me the ball, and I shouted. We made it near the sideline. This time our quarterback dropped it. The tight end pitched it back, and they threw it to me. The ball was a little high, but I knew I needed to make it.

I went up and made the grab, but when I came down, a player hit me in my left knee from the right. Another player hit me from the left in that same spot. My leg just buckled on me. It felt like it was completely destroyed. My knee was weak, and I had no stability. I kept trying to move, but I couldn't get comfortable anywhere. I counted and saw the referee come over and blow his whistle to my sideline for help. All I wanted was for my pain to go away. I didn't care about winning this game. I didn't care about the state championship. I didn't care about the scouts being impressed with my performance. Again, I just wanted the pain to stop, but it wasn't stopping.

There was silence in the loud facility. A spirit had dawned on me. Had I shattered my knee? Was my career over? Boy, did I wish this was a nightmare. Paramedics came onto the field and over to me, touching the spot that was causing the excruciating pain. My father came over to hold my hand. Coach was there shaking his head. I knew this wasn't good.

"Lord," I prayed silently, *"What are You doing?"*

What seemed like moments later I woke up in the hospital. My mother was sitting in a chair crying. My father was pacing the floor yelling, "He's gon' be okay, Pat. He's gon' be okay."

As I blinked my eyes open, my mom came over to my bed. "Oh, sweetheart!"

My dad stood behind her with his arm around her waist.

"Junior, you gon' be all right, Son. You gon' be just fine."

"Dad, what's going on? My leg hurts."

"Just lay still now. I got good and bad news, Son. It's serious, but it's not that serious that you can't hold it together, okay?"

"What's going on, Dad? Just tell me."

"It's your posterior cruciate ligament. In six to eight weeks, you'll be fine to train in somebody's camp this summer. It's nothing that you can't overcome and nothing that should make these schools less interested. We just want you to relax. You'll get healthy."

I should've known this was going to happen. With me trying to boost myself up to fit into a school. My intent might have cost me the chance to go to any school at all. A PCL tear was a pretty big deal, being in the back of the leg. Not only did it have to repair itself, but it also had to regain its strength. At least I didn't tear the ACL. Sometimes when you get hit, getting hurt was unavoidable. Thank God this wasn't an injury for surgery.

I was tired of being tough. I was tired of being strong. Balling up my fists, I just hit the hospital bed over and over. I knew that ball was too high, but I went up to try and grab it for my team. Now it might've cost me everything, putting myself out there like that. We didn't even win the game. The only good thing was seeing my parents together telling me it'd be okay.

My mom told me that a lot of my teammates had been up to the hospital, but they weren't allowing any visitors right now. I knew it was just as well. I was brokenhearted.

The next couple of days while I lay in my own bed, my parents were supportive. My mom was my nurse. My dad handled tons of calls from college scouts. I didn't know what they were saying to him about how their schools felt about me. I had a feeling of uneasiness. I wanted my dad to come in my room and tell me what was up so that I could stop speculating. Finally he did.

"Dad, what's going on? You were on the phone almost all day."

"Everybody's called. Even the teams you weren't going to go with. They were just calling to check on you. Reporters have been ringing the phones like crazy. The number-one player in the state goes down, and they wanna know if he can get back up."

"Well, I saw in the papers that Lance Shadrach is the number-one player in the state," I muttered, having a pity party.

"Come on, Son, don't be beating yourself up, okay? Lance is riding off the fact that he won the championship. If you had won that game, it'd be a totally different story."

"Do I still have as many offers as I had before going into game?" I asked my father, trying to sit up a little.

He came over and helped me slide up on a pillow. "Your mom's got you all hooked up. Cold drink, pillows stacked high. You all comfy?"

"Come on, Dad. It's not that good, huh?"

My dad spoke caringly: "Okay, Son, you wanna hear it? Most of the guys that called were worried about the injury. The offers aren't off the table, but some schools let me know they might have to go to the number-two receiver on their list. A couple of schools I haven't heard from yet, and a few coaches told me that they tried for a while to get through. You know the phones have been ringing off the hook, and I'm sure I haven't talked to everybody. We'll find the right school for you, Son. We just want you to get better first, and then everything else will fall into place."

All of a sudden, a calm came over my spirit. It was like God was speaking to me at that very moment.

I just blurted out: "Dad, don't be down. This is a good

thing. We get to see what teams really want me. You're right. I've done all I could do. I've proven myself to the fullest these last couple of seasons. If colleges wanna back down on me, then that's not where I should've gone, anyway. I really didn't know how I was going to make my decision. Maybe this was supposed to happen to me."

"Dang, Perry. You're making me see it a better way, and I've been praying all day. Mom's sure worried about you. I think God just spoke through you. I hope your team will step up soon."

"Ain't no doubt about it, Dad. The pain in my leg is subsiding. I'm trusting God to hear my needs and I'm gonna trust Him to place me in the school that's right for me. I was mad at first, but I'm getting a better perspective. Learning to trust Him with the good and bad and knowing that He can help me with both."

My dad came over to me, laid his hand on my bed and prayed.

"Lord, thank You for giving me a son who knows You. Keep my boy strong during this. Carry his burden. I'm so proud of him, Lord. And I'm so thankful that You allowed me a second chance with him. In Jesus's name we pray. Amen."

"Thanks, Dad."

"No, Son, thank you."

There wasn't really anything else to be said even though there were still uncertainties about many things in my life. I was cool with that because I had given it all to God. If He could make me and my dad start talking again, then I was convinced that God could do anything.

* * *

Two weeks had passed, and we were finally out for Christmas break. I hadn't gone too many places, just to school and back. My knee still wasn't that strong but I wasn't letting it keep me down. Justin had been taking me to school and bringing me home. Being in my condition, I wasn't able to drive.

"Where we going? I'm tired, man. Take me home," I said to Justin after school on Friday.

"I just gotta pick up something at my crib. It ain't gon' take long!" When we got to his house, he insisted I come in. "This might take a minute."

"Boy, you said it wouldn't take long."

"You want something to drink? You ain't gotta go to the bathroom?"

"Naw, I'm cool. Hurry."

"I'm just saying. I don't think it's a good idea for you to stay cramped up in a car all day. You need to stretch it and stuff."

"All right, all right," I said, since I figured he wasn't gon' let me chill.

When we stepped into his house a lot of friends popped out from everywhere, yelling, "Surprise, Perry!" or "Get Well!" I was stunned. My boys weren't there but a lot of the football players were, even Marlon. I knew he didn't care 'bout me none, and I didn't know what the catch was until I saw Tori come around the corner.

So many people came up to me asking what they could do to help me feel better. Many asked if I felt okay. I couldn't be annoyed 'cause folks cared. Then the door opened and Damarius and Cole walked in. The three of us just looked at each other. I didn't know how to respond.

Cole walked over to me and said, "You know you still my boy, right?"

Deep down I was hoping they would come. Damarius and I just slapped hands and that was enough. Right now, I knew neither of us was ready to open up. That was the way some guys handled their mess. Everything didn't have to be serious all the time. Some stuff you just had to let go.

"Yeah, we're straight, Cole," I said, as my boys checked out my leg.

"Yo mama had you all on lockdown and stuff when we called. Said you were sleeping," Damarius said jokingly.

I missed the both of them, a lot. I'd only hoped that they'd change their lifestyle. I didn't think casual sex was cool, but I couldn't judge or condemn them. I learned I just needed to pray and ask God to help.

The party, like my birthday party, came unexpected. I had to give it to Justin, though. Cars weren't all along the streets or in front of his house, and he had a spread that was out of this world.

"Man, how did you pull this off?" I asked him as I dug into some chicken wings.

"Actually, your girl Tori hooked up the food. I just had to provide the place and tell people about it."

Damarius had got the music going while people gathered around him. "Okay, okay, okay, everybody. Thank y'all for coming to show Perry that y'all care 'bout his injury. We know that he can overcome it, and eventually he'll get those millions. When he does, he better not forget his friends! But enough with the greetings. Let's get the party jumping! Where's the party at?"

People yelled back, "Over here!"

That boy was so crazy. As the party continued, I hobbled to the bathroom. I was disappointed to find it locked. Then I heard a scream and what sounded like a scuffle. When I leaned closer, I heard a familiar voice.

"You've already done this. Quit holding out on me!" It was Marlon.

"I don't wanna do this with you anymore," Tori said. "Stop!"

I banged on the door hard. "Tori! It's me, open up."

Marlon shouted back, "Perry, man, this ain't none of your business. You need to take your crippled self and go sit down. I got this. She's mine now!"

"Marlon, stop. Get off me!" I heard Tori say from behind the door.

"Marlon, man, open up the door now! I ain't playing."

Finally he did. Tori rushed into my arms, and Marlon came up to my face.

"What? Tori, you wanna give him my leftovers now? Fine, have her."

"Stand right here," I told Tori. Before he could get out of the doorway, I grabbed his collar and brought his face straight to mine. "Don't you *ever* force yourself on her again!"

"Or what you gon' do?"

I pushed him hard against the wall and said, "Boo!" The stupid boy jumped like a little girl. "Yeah. I thought so. Now force yourself on me."

"Man, whatever." And he was gone.

As soon as he left, Tori dropped herself into my arms.

"It's okay," I said as I stroked her long brown hair.

"You just don't understand. I did mess up, Perry. I did. I know he's a dog, but he hurt me."

"He won't put his hands on you no more."

"He was grabbing my waist and he wouldn't let me go," she said as the tears fell from her eyes.

"You're okay. You're safe now."

"Thanks to you. I was just praying and hoping for relief."

~ 15 ~

Loving the Outcome

"You're okay now, Tori," I said to my ex again as I comforted her. "You don't have to worry about him messing with you anymore."

She wasn't letting go of me, and her body was still shaking. I didn't want her to be terrified, so I held her tight. I repeatedly tried to convince her that she was safe.

Then she pulled back and said, "Perry, I was so wrong."

"It's okay, Tori. I gave you reason not to trust me."

"But you tried to tell me nothing happened with you and Amandi, and I didn't believe you. And then all those rumors came about you having sex with her, I just couldn't take it. Of course that was after I hooked up with Marlon, and realized I wanted to be with you."

"You don't have to tell me all this," I told her.

"I guess what I'm trying to say is I wish that we could have another chance. Tell me it's not too late for us."

I didn't even know how to respond to Tori. She had shown me some things about herself that I wasn't cool with. The whole suicide-attempt thing was a turnoff, not to mention she just up and gave it to some dude that said what she wanted to hear. I didn't know . . . I wasn't too fond of her judgment. The Tori I liked being with was stronger. Even though she was a grade younger than me in school, she always acted way more mature than me.

Now that I felt different, I didn't know how to find a way to tell her without destroying her or putting me in a bind. I wanted us to stay friends, so I chose my words carefully.

My lips caressed her forehead and I whispered, "You know you'll always gon' be special to me."

"So that's a no?"

I grabbed both of her hands, stepped back and gazed into her eyes. I wanted her to see that I cared. I wanted her to feel my grasp of sincerity. I wanted her to know I didn't have to be her man for us to be buddies.

She pleasantly surprised me when she said, "I get it. You don't have to answer right now."

"I'm sorry, but you're right. That's all I got. I don't know how deep I want us to go, but I do know I want us to be cool. If you have any problems or need anything, I'm here for you."

She came into my arms and hugged me tight. This time she felt surer and more comfortable. When we stepped out of the bathroom arm in arm, a whole bunch of our peers were yelling, standing right in front of us waiting to get in.

"Dang! What y'all doing in there?" Damarius asked.

"Boy, you so stupid."

"Give 'em room, everybody. Step back!" he said.

"Oh, my goodness, Tori, y'all back together," Ciara said as she and Briana came up to us.

But as soon as we let go of our embrace, Tori said some reversed news to her girls. "We got a special friendship."

"All right, well that's something to build on," Briana said.

Damarius punched me in the back.

"Man, what you doing?"

"Come with me, man. We need to talk."

We ended up in Justin's dining room, where I had had dinner with his family not too long ago.

"What's up?"

"I took your advice and told Ciara what was up with me."

"Well, what happened? What she say? She mad?"

"Don't stress yourself, man. She can never be mad at me. She was sorta ticked off, though, but we worked it out. I told her I was going to be faithful from now on."

"So what you gon' do about your lil' problem?" He looked at me weird. "I'm just saying."

"I know, I know. You looking out for both of us. I got some pills I have to take when I'm feeling weird down there. The doctor told me the times when I could hook up with some-body, so I've been educating myself on it. I wanna thank you for being a real friend. I do plan to change my habits before I end up with another disease. I really wanted to tell you to mind your own business, but thanks to you pushing me I got a free ride to Fort Valley."

"What!" I was fired up for my boy.

"I gotta be committed and still do well on the SAT. I gotta get rid of that F I got in government. For the most part, Coach Pugh thinks he can get me in. And he wants me to start."

"Dang, man. That's real good, D," I said to my boy.

I wouldn't want anybody else coming down on him or passing judgment. I couldn't. I realized if me and Amandi would've got down in the car a while back, ain't no telling what I would've gotten from that wild girl. But I knew I was telling Damarius what I honestly thought. I was watching out for him and Cole. I didn't have no brothers, so they filled the spot.

And speaking of Cole, I was even more excited for what God was doing 'cause Cole had apologized, too. "My girl had the abortion. She is having nightmares and stuff about peo-ple saying she killed a kid. I feel bad knowing I went through with it, too. Maybe we should have thought about adoption or tried to raise the kid ourselves. But we were selfish and tried to be tough. That's why I brought you over there. Now she saying she don't wanna have sex with me, and you know how much I love it. God found a way to punish me. I should have listened to you, Perry. Sorry man."

All three of us just laughed.

"Y'all so crazy."

Cole asked, "How's that leg, though? You know everybody been asking 'bout you."

"I'm gon' get it back straight, you know me. I'll be able to work out hard pretty soon. It will get strong again."

"Dang, boy. You gotta get better for real," Damarius said.

"As mad as we were at each other, God done worked that out. I'm sure he can do some miracles on this leg. I can see the two of y'all pushing me in the gym."

"Oh, yeah. We definitely gon' do that," Cole said.

"What about schools, though, Perry?"

"Their interest has been falling off."

"Don't stress about that, man. Their loss," Damarius told me.

"I just gotta make sure I do my part and a school and will come along," I said.

Damarius and I slapped hands. I was so glad that they were going to reevaluate their crazy lifestyles. Tori and I found a way to really be what we needed to be to each other and that was friends. Damarius was right, I did have big faith. I was proving we could do anything but fail if we trusted God.

Justin dropped me off at my house. I was totally shocked to walk in and see my parents on the couch, all into each other. My mom was all rested in my dad's arms. My dad's legs were up with his feet on the coffee table. One of his hands was rubbing her cheek and his other hand was rubbing her thigh.

I joked. "I must be in the wrong house."

"Boy, come on in here," my dad teased. "Your mom and I have been trying to work out our problems."

My mom stood up and came over to me. "Sit down."

I plopped down in the recliner. She rubbed my forehead and replied, "Your dad told me you walked in on him."

My eyes opened wide.

"Yes, I told her," my pops announced. "I told her everything about my life and how I've not been right. I need to straighten up some things, and to do that I needed to get right with the Lord."

"You done with all that, Dad?" I looked at my dad. "I'm sorry, Mom, I just need to know."

"It's okay, Son, that's a fair question. Clarissa's gone."

"What do you mean she's gone?"

He said, "I mean, not only did I end the relationship, but I also let her go."

I looked down and shook my head. My dad knew I had more questions.

"Ask what you want, Son. Talk to me, Junior."

"All right, cool," I said as my dad pushed me to share my feelings. "How we know that this is the only situation you got? Was there anybody else we don't know about? Was this lady the only one you dipped out with? I mean, because I don't know. My mom didn't deserve to be treated like that."

My mom didn't do anything when my dad dogged her like that. Okay, she might not look the way she did when they first hooked up. But then I noticed that my dad wasn't looking all that good, either. I know he didn't have those rolls in his gut twentysomething years ago that he has now.

Yeah, he had some money in his pockets. But he needed to give me more answers. I wanted to know why he did it. I wanna understand and move past it, like my mother obviously had.

"Why did you do it, Dad?"

"Honey, let me answer that," my mom said to him. "Perry, your mom hasn't done her job. I didn't have another man, but I wasn't taking care of the one I had. You're old enough to know now what I'm saying."

"Yeah, I know."

"You know," she said as she looked at my dad. I could sorta tell they wondered if I was still pure. "You should've seen the way I used to pull away from your father since your sister's been gone. I don't know. It's like my body has been doing some weird things: my oldest baby is gone, and I've been reserved. I've been a little down. I haven't really wanted to express myself to my husband the way I'm supposed to. So if he is saying that I pushed him into the arms of another, then I'm not saying I didn't."

I couldn't look at either of them at the moment. This was a lot. I only hoped they could work it out.

"We don't know what's going to happen to us in the near future, Son, but your dad and I are willing to try hard to keep our family together. We wanna be with each other."

My dad turned and kissed my mom. I had never seen my parents show affection. To see them kiss passionately was moving.

Then a key turned in the door and my sister walked in and dropped her bags on the floor. She was home from college.

"I thought this was going to be a horrible Christmas. Thank you, Lord!" she said, as she raised her hands toward the sky.

I was glad the family was happy. We ordered pizza and watched a movie. Life was coming together, and I was loving it. After the movie, the phone rang and my dad answered it.

My dad said, "Hey, Coach, how's the team doing down there at Georgia Tech?" At that point, the movie was watching itself. My mom, sister and I turned our eyes toward my dad. "Yeah, he's doing much better. Yeah, we know you guys really want him. He really is a good kid, and he'll recover 100 percent from his injury, I'll assure that. Hold on a sec."

My father could hardly contain his grin as he handed me the phone.

"Uh, Perry?" Coach Sparks asked.

"Yes, sir."

"I tried to call a couple of times but wasn't able to get through. Our chaplain told us that he saw you; and you came to one of his retreats or something."

"Yes, sir."

"He speaks highly of you. So does everyone else that I talk to. I saw the state championship game film. Sorry about your knee."

"Thank you, sir."

"Of course I was disappointed for you, but we've got some ideas about getting you well, and giving you confidence about that knee. We still want you to come here, Perry. I'm excited to have a chaplain on our campus 'cause a lot of colleges don't. On game days I wanna make sure that you have a fulfilling view on life, mentally speaking. I can't promise you how many wins or losses, but I can promise that you will have stepped into a family that will care for you similarly to how your own is carrying for you right now. Don't wanna put any pressure on you 'cause I know that you still have many opportunities, and I honestly know of other places that wanted to sign you, too. But here, we feel just as good about you today as we did before the injury. Commit here, and you won't be disappointed about being a Yellow Jacket."

"Thanks, Coach."

"All right. Hope to hear from you soon."

"Yes, sir."

After I got off the phone, we all jumped up and down.

This had been one of the schools I had been highly consider-ing before the injury, and to be one of the schools that still wanted me solidified my answer. My mom smiled warmly. No matter what happened with football she knew that at that school, I'd be okay.

"When you gon' call the man and commit?" my dad asked in a firm tone.

Giving him his dues, I looked at him and said, "Soon."

He said, "Then I support it. It's absolutely the right deci-sion. Coach Sparks is a good man. You might not get a state championship, but with his direction and your talent, Tech will make a run at another national title."

"Well, let's call him tomorrow," I said.

"Sounds good."

I could hardly sleep. I decided I needed to pray and thank God for all the crazy things he was doing. Once I did that, I went into restless slumber.

It was Christmas Eve, and I was in the holiday spirit. This semester had started off so rocky for me, but I began to un-derstand why I was here: to live for God, to win souls for Him and to put Him first. He gave me a complete perspective on how I needed to live my life and where my happiness came from. So with this being the time of year to celebrate Jesus's birth, I was back to my old joking, positive self.

With my better attitude, I felt a little stronger. I still couldn't drive, but it was cool. I was ready to cram. Tad Taylor was my first target. He'd been at my house all day up under my sister.

So I teased, "All right, now. My sister got you whipped, don't she?"

"Perry, hush!" Payton said.

Tad defended, "It's cool. Let him tease me all he wants. One day he'll understand. He just ain't found the right one yet."

Payton leaned over to her boyfriend and gave him a kiss.

"Eww!" I said. "Next time ask for privacy."

Payton saw a little toy on the couch and hurled it at me.

"Naw, I'm just kidding. I'm glad my sister has somebody like you in her life."

"Look, man. What you got planned tonight?" Tad asked me before I walked out the room.

"Y'all don't need to worry about me tonight. I don't mind hanging out with myself, it's cool."

"Oh, naw. I just wanted to know if you wanted to go to a Christmas concert. My church in Augusta is having this big thing and my cousin Savoy is singing."

Now I have to admit at first that I wasn't planning on going but when he said Savoy was gonna be there, I got interested.

"How she's been?" I asked.

"She's been good. She asked about you."

"Really?" I asked, smiling ear to ear. "I haven't talked to her since we left the retreat."

"You haven't called her or anything?" My sister put in her two cents. "Dang, boy, I thought I taught you better than that."

"Come on, now. Savoy is good people. She still got that boyfriend, right?"

I was hoping the answer would be no, but Tad wasn't sure. He just knew that they were having a few problems. The status of their relationship didn't really matter to me 'cause I knew she was asking 'bout me.

Tad and Payton were helping my mom finish decorating the house, and I was in my room thinking about Savoy. I was wondering why I hadn't called her and what would be the harm of saying hello; we were friends. I went over to my nightstand, grabbed my dingy wallet and tore it up looking for her phone numbers. She had written them on hot pink paper. I was full of joy when I saw her name and two numbers.

I reached her on her cell.

"Hey, it's Perry."

"Hello. Are you better?"

"I don't know. I haven't gotten a call from you checking on me."

I don't know why I said that, 'cause I'd been hoping that she wouldn't call me.

"You could've called me and told me 'bout it personally."

"You right. So, how you been?" I asked, really concerned.

"I think since we left the conference, I've been good. It's like nothing really matters but God. And any other problems I've had, Perry, I've just completely cleared away. Saxon and I are going to the same school."

"Oh, for real. Where y'all going?"

"Georgia Tech. Can you believe that? You know we both want to be architects. I could run track and my brother can handle the football. We may try and have our own business together building houses one day."

I just started laughing. This was a trip! We'd chosen the same school.

"Have you decided where you want to go?"

"That's why I'm laughing so hard, 'cause I'm going there, too."

"You serious?" she asked, almost screaming excitedly.

"So, how is everything with your boyfriend?" I held my breath.

"We decided to be friends. I'm thinking about a few other things these days."

I did a dance when she said that. White, black, Chinese, Puerto Rican—I didn't care as long as he was gone. I knew I really liked her.

"Um, I'm coming to your church tonight to hear you sing."

"You are?"

"Yeah. Tad invited me. I didn't know you could blow."

"I can do a few things."

"And after, I might need a ride home."

"I could take you home," she said.

"Cool," I said, happy she offered.

"So it's a date, Mr. Skky? Does a date sound too formal?"

"No, a date sounds just fine. See you this evening."

Before I could say anything else she hung up. Boy, she had me! There was something mysterious about her.

Later that evening as I sat beside my sister and heard Savoy sing "Ave Maria" I was in awe. She was really good.

Saxon came up to me and said, "So I hear you and I are wearing the white and gold?"

"Yeah, man. Congratulations. I thought you were going to a South Carolina school," I said.

"Oh, well. I like Tech's academic track and Coach Sparks is a good guy. And if my sister can come, too on a full scholarship, it works. Plus, we'll be there with the best quarterback I know. Shadrach committed, too. What about you? I thought you were going to follow your sister to Georgia?"

"Too late with my injury, they signed another cat."

"Oh, the boy from Florida? Please! He ain't got the skills you and I have."

We slapped hands. I got a chance to really chat with him for a bit. Then he just stared at me.

He said, "My sister . . . need I say more?"

"I hear you, man. I hear ya," I said as we walked over to his folks.

After chatting with his parents for a bit, Savoy came over. Soon she and I headed off. We headed over to Applebee's.

"You looked so beautiful," I said to her as I gazed into her eyes and held her hand.

"Why, thank you. You're handsome yourself."

We were eating hamburgers and sharing a chocolate milkshake. If Damarius and Cole would've seen me, they would've called me a punk. But something happened to me. Something I couldn't explain. I'd waited on God for everything, and He was working it out. My family life, partners, school, and now a girl sweeter than what I could ever imagine. I reached out and touched her face and cupped the softness in my hands.

"What are you thinking about?" she asked.

"I'm just thankful right now. Christmas is tomorrow. It's just like you said over the phone, since that conference, it seems like I've had nothing but peace. I've been happy." She took my hand and gripped it tight. "Savoy, I ain't even gon' lie to you—things have been crazy. Me and my girl just wanna be friends, too. I did some stuff that was wrong this past semester. God has worked in my life in every situation. He means something to me. Can I be honest?" She nodded. "I wanna be with you. I want you to put your face to mine, and I want to leave this place and . . ." She blushed. "But a bigger part of me wants to please God even more than I want that fantasy. I want to make right decisions, you know."

She squeezed my hand and we talked about how we felt about our budding feelings for each other and the strong emotions we felt for God. I'd grown a lot and I wouldn't trade my experiences for anything. In all the mess I had going on this semester, I did something with it. I gave it to God and now I'm loving the outcome.

Perry Skky Jr., Book 1:

PRIME CHOICE

Stephanie Perry Moore

ABOUT THIS GUIDE

The following questions are intended to
enhance your group's reading of
PERRY SKKY JR.: PRIME CHOICE
by Stephanie Perry Moore.

DISCUSSION QUESTIONS

1. Perry Skky Jr. loves God, but also wants to make his relationship with his longtime girlfriend, Tori, physical. Is the spirit or the flesh leading him in the beginning of the book? What do you do when physical attraction heats up in your life?

2. Perry breaks off their relationship when he doesn't get what he wants. What do you do when things don't go your way? When should a relationship end?

3. At a party, Perry has many girls willing to meet his desires. Do you think he handled the advances correctly? What are ways to fight off temptation?

4. Perry and his father don't have the best relationship at the beginning of the book. Do you speak to your parents the way Perry talks to his dad? What does God's word say about children obeying their parents?

5. Perry's friends are sexually active. What are the two main problems Damarius and Cole encounter in this area? What are other consequences to having premarital sex?

6. Perry is the top football player in his area. Do you think he handles the pressure well? What are things you can do to stay grounded when things are going great in your life?

7. Tori, Perry's ex-girlfriend, is so devastated their relationship is over that she wants to end her life. How does Perry help her when he finds out she is severely depressed? What are ways you can help a friend get through their pain?

8. Perry confronts his dad about his extra marital affair. Do you think he should have stayed out of it? How can you help your parents have the type of relationship God wants for them?

9. Perry hurts his leg during a big game. Do you think he had the right attitude about his dire situation? Why do you think God allows us to go through disappointments?

10. Perry gets a new girlfriend, Savoy, and finally realizes that he wants to honor God in his dating relationship. Do you think Perry and Savoy will keep this goal in future books? What are ways to keep the Lord in the middle of your dating relationships?

Start Your Own Book Club

Courtesy of the PERRY SKKY JR. series

ABOUT THIS GUIDE

The following is intended to help you get
the Book Club you've always wanted
up and running!
Enjoy!

Start Your Own Book Club

A Book Club is not only a great way to make friends, but it is also a fun and safe environment for you to express your views and opinions on everything from fashion to teen pregnancy. A Teen Book Club can also become a forum or venue to air grievances and plan remedies for problems.

The People

To start, all you need is yourself and at least one other person. There's no criteria for who this person or persons should be other than a desire to read and a commitment to read and discuss during a certain time frame.

The Rules

People tend to disagree with each other, cut each other off when speaking, and take criticism personally. So, there should be some ground rules:

1. Do not attack people for their ideas or opinions.

2. When you disagree with a book club member on a point, disagree respectfully. This means that you do not denigrate another person for their ideas. There shouldn't be any name calling or saying, "That's stupid!" Instead, say, "I can respect your position, however, I feel differently."

3. Back up your opinions with concrete evidence, either from the book in question or life in general.

4. Allow every one a turn to comment.

5. Do not cut a member off when the person is speaking. Respectfully wait your turn.

6. Critique only the idea (and do so responsibly; again,

simply saying, "That's stupid!" is not allowed). Do not criticize the person.

7. Every member must agree to and abide by the ground rules.

Feel free to add any other ground rules you think might be necessary.

The Meeting Place

Once you've decided on members, and agreed to the ground rules, you should decide on a place to meet. This could be the local library, the school library, your favorite restaurant, a bookstore, or a member's home. Remember, though, if you decide to hold your sessions at a member's home, the location should rotate to another member's home for the next session. It's also polite for guests to bring treats when attending a Book Club meeting at a member's home. If you choose to hold your meetings in a public place, always remember to ask the permission of the librarian or store manager. If you decide to hold your meetings in a local bookstore, ask the manager to post a flyer in the window announcing the Book Club to attract more members if you so desire.

Timing is Everything

Teenagers of today are all much busier than teenagers of the past. You're probably thinking, "Between chorus rehearsals, the Drama Club, and oh yeah, my job, when will I ever have time to read another book that doesn't feature Romeo and Juliet!" Well, there's always time, if it's time well-planned and time planned ahead. You and your Book Club can decide to meet as often or as little as is appropriate for your bustling schedules. *Once a month* is a favorite option. *Sleepover Book Club* meetings—if you're open to excluding one gender—is also a favorite option. And in this day of high-tech, savvy teens, *Internet Discussion Groups* are also an appealing option. Just choose what's right for you!

Well, you've got the people, the ground rules, the place, and the time. All you need now is a book!

The Book

Choosing a book is the most fun. PRIME CHOICE is of course an excellent choice, and since it's part of a series, you won't soon run out of books to read and discuss. Your Book Club can also have comparative discussions as you compare the first book, PRIME CHOICE, to the second, PRESSING HARD, and so on.

But depending upon your reading appetite, you may want to veer outside of the Perry Skky Jr. series. That's okay. There are plenty of options, many of which you will be able to find under the Dafina Books for Young Readers Program in the coming months.

But don't be afraid to mix it up. Nonfiction is just as good as fiction and a fun way to learn about from where we came without just using a history text book. Science fiction and fantasy can be fun, too!

And always research the author. You might find the author has a website where you can post your Book Club's questions or comments. You can correspond with Stephanie Perry Moore by visiting her website, www.stephanieperrymoore.com. She can sit in on your meetings, either in person, or on the phone, and this can be a fun way to discuss the book as well!

The Discussion

Every good Book Club discussion starts with questions. PRIME CHOICE, as will every book in the Perry Skky Jr. series, comes along with a Reading Group Guide for your convenience, though of course, it's fine to make up your own. Here are some sample questions to get started:

1. What's this book all about anyway?

2. Who are the characters? Do we like them? Do they remind us of real people?

3. Was the story interesting? Were real issues of concern to you examined?

4. Were there details that didn't quite work for you or ring true?

5. Did the author create a believable environment—one that you could visualize?

6. Was the ending satisfying?

7. Would you read another book from this author?

Record Keeper

It's generally a good idea to have someone keep track of the books you read. Often libraries and schools will hold reading drives where you're rewarded for having read a certain number of books in a certain time period. Perhaps, a pizza party awaits!

Get Your Teachers and Parents Involved

Teachers and parents love it when kids get together and read. So involve your teachers and parents. Your Book Club may read a particular book where it would help to have an adult's perspective as part of the discussion. Teachers may also be able to include what you're doing as a Book Club in the classroom curriculum. That way books you love to read such as PRIME CHOICE can find a place in your classroom alongside the books you don't love to read as much.

Resources

To find some new favorite writers, check out the following resources. Happy reading!

Young Adult Library Services Association
http://www.ala.org/ala/yalsa/yalsa.htm

Carnegie Library of Pittsburgh
Hip-Hop!
Teen Rap Titles
http://www.carnegielibrary.org/teens/read/booklists/ teenrap.html

TeensPoint.org
What Teens Are Reading?
http://www.teenspoint.org/reading_matters/book_list.asp? sort=5&list=274

Teenreads.com
http://www.teenreads.com/

Sacramento Public Library
Fantasy Reading for Kids
http://www.saclibrary.org/teens/fantasy.html

Book Divas
http://www.bookdivas.com/

Meg Cabot Book Club
http://www.megcabotbookclub.com/

Stay tuned for the next book in this series
PRESSING HARD,
available September 2007 wherever books are sold.
Until then, satisfy your Perry Skky Jr. craving
with the following excerpt from the next installment.

ENJOY!

~ 1 ~
Grooving too Much

"**Y**ou a punk. A little mama's boy. That's why you won't have a drink," Damarius taunted as I helped him carry beer from the car to his house for the New Year's Eve jam he was about to host.

I was tired of it. He could call me whatever he wanted to. Say whatever he wanted to say. I didn't care. He wasn't going to pressure me into doing something I wasn't ready to do.

"Come on, Cole," Damarius said, looking to our friend for backup. "You need to admit it too. That's what you think of his tail. Do you think he all that? He hadn't never even had a piece, drank a little nip or smoked a joint. Dang! Perry ain't no real man yet."

I wanted to take one of those six packs and bust him across the head with it. But because we were late setting things up, I let it go. Cole, standing in the back, spoke up.

"All right you two. Kiss and make-up," Cole said before Damarius and I went our separate ways.

It didn't take the place long to fill up. Not only were there a lot of kids from my school in the house, but folks from all over Augusta were showing up. I felt sort of bad that I didn't call my girl Savoy, but honestly the whole commitment thing was scaring me a bit. I didn't want to feel pressured into a relationship with her. I hadn't seen her since Christmas night, but I thought about her all the time.

As I walked around scanning the crowd, I thought about Damarius accusing me and his calling me a punk. So if a brother didn't get high or get wasted, then he wasn't cool? I knew Damarius was just jealous. I didn't need anything to make me feel good about me. I was high off of life. College coaches were always trying to persuade me to change my choice from going to Georgia Tech. Girls were always trying to get with me. Brothers always wanting me to attend their functions or just to hang out with them to raise their stock with the ladies. I had it like that.

At that moment, none of that meant a thing to me. I wanted respect from my boy. Was proving to him that I could handle alcohol the only way I could get him off my back? I don't know why I was letting him get to me. Maybe I should just pray about it. After all, I had learned this year that if I just give it to Him, He'd make my situation better.

Deep down I had to admit that I felt as if I was at the sidelines looking on. I peered in like I was watching this stuff on the TV or something. Maybe I had issues and I needed to release, let go, and get down.

When I stepped into the hallway, I saw Jaboe, a thug from down the block. Jaboe was a high school dropout who should have graduated with my sister's class two years ago, but he started selling drugs. He told the world that he could make way more money hustling than he ever could the legitimate way.

"Hey man. I'm good for it! You ain't gotta jack me up like that," Damarius told Jaboe as the thug grabbed him by his collar and squeezed it tight.

What did my boy get himself into? It was hard for me to believe that he was doing drugs. The pressure of wanting to get into a major college had given my buddy a new perspective on right from wrong.

"I want some bills, boy. I don't want no change," Jaboe said as he slung the coins in his hand to the ground. "You got all these folks in here for free. You better start charging some money next time you have a party 'cause I want my paper. If I don't get it next week, not only will you be cut off from the stash," he said as he took a knife out of his pocket and put it to Damarius' face, "but you know what else is next."

Damarius tried talking his way of out the problem. "All right, dude. Ease up! I'ma get yo' money. Give me a little credit. You know I'm good for it."

I had no idea that my boy was smoking more than cigarettes. No wonder his grades were slipping.

Regardless of how he felt about me, I had to stop him from messing his life up. Like Reverend McClep preached at church the last Sunday, I was my brother's keeper. I wasn't going to let Damarius go down like that. I saw Jaboe pull out a dime bag and I quickly intercepted it, as if I was a defensive back on the field or something and tossed it back up in his face. "He doesn't want that," I said to Jaboe. I looked over his shoulder at the two guys with him. One had cornrows with even parts going down to the back of his head and a grill, and the other dude was thicker than Mr. T himself. They stepped toward me, but I wasn't backing down. I didn't care how long Damarius had been messing around with that stuff. It was going to end today.

"Come on, Perry. What's up? You crazy? This is business," Damarius said to me.

"Is there a problem?" Jaboe asked his eyes threatening.

"No, man there ain't no problem," Damarius said stepping in between us.

"Like D said, no problem. He just don't need your stuff. So thanks for coming," I said pointing to the front door.

"What's up Damarius? You gonna let him talk for you? Or a betta question, you gonna let him talk to me like that?" Jaboe pulled up his sweater and showed us he was packing.

Throwing my hands up, I said, "I don't mean no disrespect, Jaboe. Look, he just don't need it, all right?"

"Yeah, I hear you." He laughed and dropped his top, concealing the weapon again. "Cool, I ain't trying to push my stuff off on anybody, but I do want my money."

"You'll get it. Soon, man," Damarius promised.

Jaboe and his gangster boys left. Damarius tried to go off on me about the whole thing.

Getting in my face, he said, "Man! What's up? Are you crazy? You'll mess up your whole life fooling getting in Jaboe's way."

I couldn't believe he tried to play me instead of thank me. "You need to pay him the little money you owe him and leave him alone before you end up like him on the corner somewhere. He's reduced to hiding out from the cops and bullying folks into giving him dollars."

"You don't know what you just did, Perry. Stay out of my business," he said, shaking his head as he walked past me to join the crowd in the living room. I was just about to leave the party when I heard Damarius announce over the DJ's system, "Hey y'all! Hey y'all! Y'all know my boy Perry here don't drink, right?"

What he was doing? Why he was calling me out like that?

"But it's New Year's Eve, and we want him to have a little fun, right y'all?" The crowd started chanting, "Yeaaa Perry! Drink! Drink! Drink!"

I went over to him and questioned him "What's up with this?"

"You all up in my business! You can't knock what I enjoy until you try it. Was I right earlier, Perry? Are you a punk?"

Without even thinking, I took the beer out of his hand, twisted off the top, and gulped it down. I didn't even have time to decide if I liked the taste or not. A random guy from the crowd ran up to me with another one. I wasn't no punk. Damarius was not about to play me like that. I had twisted off the cap and chugged that one down, too.

"Drink! Drink! Drink! Drink!" folks called out.

"Can you handle one more, big boy?" Damarius dared.

Cole came up said, "Man, that's enough. What you trying to do to him, D?"

"I can handle it. I'll show you it ain't all that. Give me another one." All I could hear was more chanting from the crowd when I drank the next brew.

After a few minutes I was feeling a little light-headed. But it was all good. Someone handed me another one with the top already off. I couldn't tell if someone had drunk out of it or not, but it really didn't matter. I drank it down, and when I was done, the crowd yelled and screamed louder than I could remember fans did at any football game I'd ever played in. I was feeding off of it. A couple of girls came up to me and got close: one in the front and one in the back. They swayed their hips from left to right, and my hips started moving too. Oh, the party was on.

Damarius came up to me. "Dang, man. You can hold your stuff. All right. All right. My bad." He laughed and walked away.

After a couple of dances, I went up to the DJ and started trying to spin records, which I have no skills with at all on a regular day. But being a little intoxicated, nobody couldn't tell me that I wasn't the life of the party. The sad thing was that I couldn't go anywhere without the two girls, Q and Jo, following me. It was cute, but I was getting tired of them.

"You know what? Y'all gotta give a brother some space. Dang, I can't even dance with nobody else."

They looked as if I had hurt their feelings.

"I'm sorry. I'm just being honest."

"You all right boy?" Damarius said as he came over to me and handed me another beer. "I thought you wanted this? I didn't want you to have to look for it."

Cole grabbed it out of my hand. "No, no, D. He done had enough for real."

"Whatcha mean, I done had enough?"

"Tell 'em. Perry, tell 'em. You feeling good right about now, right?" Damarius said.

"Good? I feel the same. Whatcha talking about?"

I was so out of it, I didn't even know what Damarius was talking about.

"Nawh, Perry," Cole said, turning away.

"Man, give me that beer!" I grabbed the beer out of my boy's hand spilling some of it on the floor. Sipping the beer, I stepped around my boys so I could get back to dancing.

I stopped and had to blink my eyes a couple of times when I saw my ex, Tori, standing in the middle of a crowd. She still looked as fine as she always did. Her hair was all done up, her nails were manicured just right, and she was wearing this cute little pink number that hugged her body just right.

"What's up girl, dang? A brother can't get no love."

She yanked my hand and pulled me down the hall. She pushed me into Damarius's bedroom and shut the door.

"Uhh ha. What's up? You wanna give yourself to me now? I just asked for hug. I didn't know you wanted to give it up."

"Perry, I love you too much to see you act like this. What's going on?"

"What you talking about, dang! You pulled me up in here. I don't need no girl giving me a hard time by telling me what to do. We don't go together no more, and I guess I should be glad of that."

"You making a fool of yourself tonight, okay."

"Man, I'm the life of this joint."

"No, people are looking at you and staring at you because

you are tripping over yourself. Drool is coming out of your mouth. It's clear you can't hold alcohol."

"Girl, shut up. Leave me alone. Bye. Get out. I'm sorry I asked for some love. I got another girl, dang. She's prettier than you."

The moment I said that, I wanted to take my words back, but I knew that wasn't possible because Tori had heard me. Her face looked devastated. I felt bad. I didn't mean to hurt her. I wasn't trying to feel horrible, but the alcohol was speaking.

"You got somebody else?"

"Forget it. Forget it. I just need to be alone."

"I mean, you just said it! You said you got somebody else! Talk to me! Tell me! Is it somebody at our school? Is it somebody I know? We haven't been broke up but a couple of months, and you already got another girlfriend?"

"I ain't said I had another girlfriend. Dang. Y'all females be tripping."

"I'm not tripping. I should have expected it. I mean, everywhere I go, girls are telling me I'm stupid for letting you go and not giving it up. If they not telling me that, they telling me they plan to satisfy you. So hey, I'm not surprised. I might as well have a drink with you," she said as she came over trying to get what was left in my bottle.

"Go on now. You don't need this. Seriously. Look, look!" I said as I shoved her to the side.

I didn't mean to push her, but again, I didn't have complete control of my faculties. What was supposed to be just a little push in my mind at the time, moved her half way across the room towards the door.

"Okay. Fine. I get it. You don't have to hurt me worse than you already have, okay." She opened the door and dashed out.

After she had gone out, I stood in my spot staring at the

opened door all upset and confused. Minutes later, I realized what I had done, and I wanted to go after her, but I began to feel a terrible burning sensation in my chest. What was going on?

I couldn't understand why I was having such horrible physical pain. It was like I was having a heart attack or something. I couldn't even make it to Damarius' bed. I fell straight to the floor. I couldn't breathe. It felt like I was going to die.

The only thing I could do was pray: *"Lord, I'm sorry. You gotta help me, though. I was stupid to drink. Being pressured and all. Yeah, I gotta admit it felt good for a minute, but right now, I feel worse than as if three linebackers tackled me. Please Lord, please."*

I couldn't even pray anymore. I looked up at Damarius' light that was circling around and around in his room thinking about all the hopes and dreams I had for myself, I wondered if this was going to be the end. Stupidity might have done me in. Maybe Tori was right about me thinking I was cool. I had not only hurt her feelings, but also I'd probably made a complete idiot out of myself. All of a sudden, I heard the door open. I didn't know who it was, but I certainly didn't want them to see me unable to keep my composure. But there was nothing I could do about that. Everything in me was hurting.

"Perry man, what's up? What's up?" Cole yelled out as he rushed to my side.

"I don't feel good, man." I was so happy to see him.

"See. I told Damarius you didn't need all that beer."

"Man, what am I suppose to do? My chest is burning for real."

"You gotta take deep breaths."

"You ever felt like this?"

"I gotta get you some water."

"Water? That's gonna help?"

"I'll be right back. Just hold on."

My boy left and it seemed like it was taking him forever to come back. Every way that I moved was wrong because it didn't offer any relief. *Why did teenagers drink?* I started asking myself. At first I could feel it. It was some pleasure in it. It made me feel good, confident, and larger than life. Now here I was, helpless. When I heard the door open again, I yelled, "Call the ambulance."

"See, I told you he was hurting." Cole said to Damarius.

"He'll be all right. Just give him the daggone water. Boy, you can't hold nothing."

I drank the water and took deep breaths as they helped me onto Damarius' bed.

"You just need to rest and relax."

"I still don't feel good y'all for real."

"Dag! I gotta bring the party in here. Nobody gonna believe this. He can't hold his own."

I didn't even care at that moment. But I heard Cole taking up for me.

I laid in that bed for the next five minutes vowing to the Lord that I would never ever go over the top with alcohol again if he let me come out alive from this situation. I thought about my parents, and how this would let them down. They had raised me better than that, even though I had been pushed by my peers to do stuff all my life. I'd always been the leader applying positive peer pressure. But here I was caught up in the wrong mess. I was trying to keep Damarius from smoking his brains away, and he turns around and pushes me to put something I don't need into my body. I now knew none of this was worth it. Trying to impress people. Trying to be in the in-crowd. All that stuff was silly. I had to stay in my lane and run my race. I couldn't let nobody ever pressure me again. As I took a deep breath and watched my chest rise higher and higher, I hated that I was grooving too much.